DOMESTIC DIFFERENCES

LOVE CAN CHANGE A FAMILY

WRITTEN BY
ANTHONY HARRIS

Inspired Forever Book Publishing
Dallas, Texas

Inspired Forever Book Publishing™
"Words with Lasting Impact"
Dallas, Texas
(888) 403-2727

Printed in the United States of America

Library of Congress Control Number: 2019914576

ISBN-13: 978-1-948903-15-8

ISBN-10: 1-948903-15-6

DEDICATION PAGE

To Constance—a loving mother, daughter, and sister, whose encouraging words and faith have guided me on my path.

A loving thank you to my son, Christopher McClendon, for his contribution in writing and for his poetry that helped me complete my first book.

Ring, ring, ring, ring.

"Hello?"

"Hi, Mrs. Harris. Is AJ home?"

"No, he hasn't made it in yet. May I ask who is calling?"

"It's Connie. Ma'am, please turn on the news."

"Why? What's going on?" Anthony's mom asks.

"Your husband's bank just got robbed."

"Are you sure it's the bank my husband works at?"

"Yes ma'am. My mom works across the street. I was on my way to pick her up, but the police have the street blocked."

"Do you know if anyone is hurt?"

"No ma'am. The police wouldn't tell us anything."

* * *

"This is Linda Jameson with Action 4 News, reporting live at Chase Bank here on Greenville Avenue, where two men have just robbed and shot two bank tellers. No word at this time if any others have been harmed. We will bring you more as this story develops . . ."

CHAPTER ONE

THE MCKINNEY TAVERN
LATER THAT DAY

Anthony Sr. loses his job of fifteen years as a bank manager due to a bank robbery in which he didn't follow protocol.

Instead of going home, he goes to a sports bar to clear his head. After drinking his fourth shot of brandy and Coke, Anthony Sr. stumbles out to his car, lays his head on the steering wheel, and wonders, "How can I explain this to my family?" As he raises his head, he pounds on the steering wheel in anger. He reaches an empty hand over to the ignition switch but realizes he isn't holding his keys. "Damn. Must have left them inside," he mutters, followed by a sigh.

Anthony Sr. stumbles back into the bar, bumping into patrons as he approaches the counter. The spot where he'd been sitting has already been cleared, and there's no sign of his keys. With slurred speech, he says, "Hey. Hey, you," and points a finger at the man behind the counter.

The bartender looks over pointedly as if to say, "What the hell you want now?" But instead, he says, "Sir, can I help you by calling you a cab? You appear to be a little drunk."

Anthony Sr. replies, "No! What you can do is give me my keys that I left in here."

The bartender replies, "Sir, I'm sorry, but I can't allow you to drive. I won't give you the keys. However, I can call you a ride."

Anthony Sr. pounds on the table, demanding his keys. The bartender insists that he leave, telling him, "I don't want to call the cops, but if you don't calm down, I will have to."

"I'm not drunk—hell, I'm not even tipsy yet. Man, look, I just lost my job after fifteen years and don't know how to tell my wife."

"I'm sorry to hear that, but I still can't let you drive in your current condition. If you want, you can relax in the corner booth for a while. Sir, look at yourself. You can barely stand on your own." The bartender places his hand on Anthony Sr.'s shoulder as if to steady him.

Anthony Sr. in turn pushes him away and says, "I don't need to relax. I need my damn keys." He then pushes past the bartender and stumbles around behind the bar in search of his keys.

"Sir, you can't be back here. If you don't leave now, I will be forced to call the police."

Anthony Sr. ignores his threat, asking, "Where the fuck are my keys?" as he begins to rifle through drawers.

"I've had enough. I'm calling the police . . ."

***

"911—do you need ambulance, fire, or rescue?"

"Ma'am, I need the police here at the McKinney Tavern."

"What is the problem, sir?"

"I have a drunk customer out of control, and he refuses to leave."

"Does he have any weapons at this time, sir?"

"No, but he is behind my bar, going through the drawers, and I do have a gun hidden back there."

"Sir, do you have any security that can calm the situation till police arrive?"

"No, I've never had the use for them."

In the background, Anthony Sr. screams, "Where the fuck are my keys? I will break every bottle in this motherfucker!"

The operator clearly can hear the commotion of bottles breaking, as she asks, "Sir, is everything okay?"

"No, he's throwing bottles."

Patrons begin screaming and trying to get out of the way of the bottles being hurled across the room.

"Sir, the police have been notified and are on the way."

"Please tell them to hurry. He's tearing up the place!"

***

Just as AJ begins telling his mom that he is thinking of going to the University of Arkansas Pine Bluff after he graduates high school, the phone rings.

AJ picks it up. "Hello?"

"Hello, sir. Is Janice Harris there?"

AJ replies, "Yes . . . may I ask who is calling?"

"This is Officer Young of the Dallas Police Department. May I speak with Mrs. Harris?"

"Mom, telephone. It's the police."

"*Again?*" She grabs the phone. "Yes, this is Janice Harris."

"Hi, ma'am, this is Officer Young. I'm calling on behalf of your husband, Mr. Harris. He is being arrested and wanted to know if you could come get his vehicle."

"What is he being arrested for?" she asks with a familiar sigh.

"He is being arrested for disorderly conduct and assault at this time. He will see a judge in the morning for a bail amount. If you can't come down and get his vehicle, it will be towed tonight. It's at the McKinney Tavern on McKinney Avenue."

"I'll have my neighbor bring me there to pick it up. I can be there in twenty minutes."

"Okay, ma'am. I'll let the bartender know you are on your way. He has the keys."

"Yes sir, and thank you for calling."

AJ crosses his arms as his mom hangs up the phone. "Mom, let me guess—Dad has been arrested. *Again.*"

"Anthony, don't do that."

"Do what?" AJ asks in disgust.

"Stop being sarcastic," Janice replies as she removes a pot from the stove.

"I'm not! It's just that he goes to jail every few months. I wish they would just keep him."

"Don't say that."

"Well, it's true, and every time he gets out, he blames you for him going to jail. Besides, Mom, I'm getting tired of him putting his hands on you when he gets angry."

"Anthony, he just has a lot to deal with at his job."

"Damn it, Mom, stop making excuses for him. He has no right—no matter how tough or long his day was—to hit you. I'm sorry for cursing, but I can't stand how he treats us."

"You don't think I'm tired of it too?" she asks, her shoulders slumped in defeat. "I just don't know what to do. I've tried telling him he needs to get help for his anger, but that makes him even angrier."

"Mom, you can start by not bailing him out this time."

"I can't let him stay in there. What about his job? He'll lose it, and we can't afford to have no income right now."

"If that's all it's going to take to get rid of him—hell, Mom, I'll get a job after school."

"No, you will not."

"But, Mom—"

"No *buts*, Anthony. You stay focused on school. I'll find a way to deal with your father. I have to go pick up his car before it gets towed. I'll be back shortly. Finish cooking dinner, will you?"

AJ relents. "Okay, Mom, I will."

***

When AJ's mom leaves for the tavern, AJ calls Connie to vent about the situation.

Connie answers the phone and immediately detects a tremble in AJ's voice. She can tell something is wrong.

"Hi, AJ. What's wrong? And don't tell me nothing. I can hear it in your voice."

"It's my dad. He's been arrested again. This is his fifth time in seven months. I hope they keep him this time."

"What did he do?" Connie asks.

"I'm not sure, but the police called my mom. Why does he keep putting her through this? I wish he would just leave us alone." He drops down onto the couch.

"AJ, calm down. You are about to go off to college—then you won't have to worry about him anymore."

"I'm having second thoughts about leaving. I can't leave her here with him."

"I'm sure your mom can take care of herself. Besides, you think she's going to let you mess up your future?" There's a pause and then some muffled background noise; then Connie says, "AJ, my mom is about to go to work. When I drop her off, I'm coming over there."

"You don't have to. I'll be okay."

"You are my best friend, and I can't sit here and let you deal with this alone."

***

As Connie approaches AJ's house, she sees him sitting on the porch. Before she can pull in the driveway, he heads toward her and slides into the passenger seat.

"Can we just leave and go somewhere?" he asks. "I need to get away from this house for a while, just to clear my head."

"Sure. Where do you want to go?"

"Anywhere, as long as it's not here," AJ responds.

Connie shifts the car into drive and pulls away from his house. "Do you want to talk about what's going on in your head?"

"I can't stand him." AJ sits in silence for a minute before speaking again. "I know he's my dad . . . but sometimes I wish he wasn't. He hits my mom for any reason at all. I'm scared that when he gets out of jail, he's gonna do it again, and if he does, I don't know what I might do."

"Do you remember any good times with your dad and mom?"

AJ answers quickly, a memory already on his mind. "Sure. There was a time I came home from school, and I could hear the radio before I made it to the door. I started running, because usually he would turn up the radio so the neighbors wouldn't hear them fighting, but this time when I made it inside, they were slow dancing. My mom had a big smile, and my dad asked me if I would like to dance with my mother. He took out his recorder and taped us. We danced for what seemed like hours."

Connie smiles softly. "You see, AJ, not all of your dad's actions have been bad. Those are the times you need to remind him of. I don't know what happened, 'cause I don't live with you guys, but something terrible must have happened that your father would do the things he does. I'm not making excuses for him—what he is doing is wrong on all levels. Have you tried to talk to Ms. Allie about what's going on?

"Ms. Allie, the school counselor? *Hell* no!"

"Why not? She may be able to help you and your family."

"Ms. Allie is nice and all, but I don't want her to know my family's business."

"AJ, she is there to help us whenever we have a problem, and you, sir, have a huge one," Connie insists.

"Maybe you are right . . . but how do you even begin to bring something like this up?"

"I'm not sure, but I know you really need to. If you'd like, I could go with you Monday."

"I'm not sure I'm ready to do that just yet."

AJ's phone begins to ring just as they pull up to the corner store.

"Damn, it's my mom. I don't want to talk to her right now."

"Just answer it," Connie says. "She probably just made it back home and noticed you were gone."

"Okay, I'll see what she wants." He answers the call, with Connie leaning over to listen. "Hi, Mom."

"Anthony, where are you?"

"I'm at the store with Connie. I'll be home later. I put the food in the oven to keep it warm for you."

"Thanks, but I wish you would have called and let me know you were leaving."

"I would have, but you left your phone on the counter."

"Anyway, your dad—" his mom begins to say.

"Mom, please, I don't want to talk about him right now," AJ interrupts.

"Okay, I'll let you go and hang out with your friend, and we will talk about him later."

"Yes ma'am. Talk to you later. Bye, Mom."

Connie leans back. "Told you she was worried about you!"

"Oh, hush. You don't always have to be right, you know."

"But I am!" she says with a laugh.

"Girl, do you want anything from this store?"

"Sure, bring me a Little Debbie snack back."

"Okay, I'll get you one."

As AJ walks into the store, his phone starts to ring again. He answers, "Hello?"

"This is a twenty-second free call from an inmate at Lew Sterrett Department of Corrections, if you accept."

Before the operator can continue, AJ hangs up. Upon getting back in the car, he asks, "Can you believe that stupid ass just tried to call me?"

"Who?" Connie asks as she backs the car out of the parking spot.

"My dad!"

"Well, what did he say?"

"I hung up before he was put through."

"Now why would you do that?"

"I have nothing to say to him." AJ leans back in his seat and crosses his arms.

Connie sighs loudly. "AJ, don't be that way. After all, he is still your father."

"There's a difference in being my father and being my dad. Right now he is neither. As far as I'm concerned, he's just a sperm donor."

Connie covers her mouth and lets out a slight laugh, then quickly says, "I'm not laughing at you, but that was kind of funny."

"That's how I feel about him at this point."

"Have you been thinking about what I said?"

"Which was . . . ?"

"Talking to Ms. Allie."

AJ shrugs. "I'm not sure how to open up about this. I will, however, take you up on going with me—just not Monday, though."

"When, then? You should talk to her before things gets worse."

"How much worse can they get? I mean, he's a drunk, and he beats on my mom."

"When did he start acting this way?"

"A few years ago was when I first noticed. It started one night when they had some friends over. He was being rude after a few drinks, so their friends left. My mom started cleaning up, but he wanted to go to bed. When she said she wasn't ready, he cursed at her and demanded she come to bed. She then told him to take his drunk ass to bed, and before I knew it, he had punched her in the mouth. She flew over the table. I pushed past him to get to her. When I got to her, there was blood all over her face. I was so mad—I wanted to kill him. I guess he knew what I was thinking 'cause he said, 'Boy, if you're even thinking about jumping, please do.' I just grabbed a towel and began trying to help my mom. He said, 'I don't need this shit,' and stormed out the door. I ran to lock it and called the police."

"Wow, you have been through a lot . . ."

AJ continues, "After the police got there, I tried to tell them what happened, but I was shaking so bad I couldn't even talk. They pretty much knew what happened after seeing the house wrecked. They rushed my mom to the hospital. By the time I got there, she was in surgery. They told me that her jaw was broken and that they had to wire her mouth shut."

"Oh my God! I'm so sorry that you and your mom are going through all of this. I've known you for four years—why haven't you ever told me things were this bad?" Connie gently touches his arm in sympathy.

"You always seem so upbeat—sorry, wrong choice of words." He tries rephrasing his thoughts. "Well, I try to put on this front so that nobody knows the truth about my homelife. I've been dealing with it this long without anyone knowing."

"But, AJ, you should have talked to someone long ago."

"Yeah, you're right. You know, he showed up at the hospital the next day."

"Did he get arrested?"

"Yeah, but he was out within a week. He was put on probation for a year and ordered to do sixty hours of community service."

"That's *all*?" Connie exclaims.

"Yeah, and he was allowed to come back home. After that, my mom was so scared of him that she would spend all day trying to please him so that he wouldn't get pissed."

"I wouldn't know what to do if I had to live like that."

"Connie, be grateful that you don't." AJ hesitates and then says, "You know, I started writing poetry about domestic violence, hoping that my parents would see it and realize how it is affecting me. I would leave it lying around so they would take notice and read it, but they never did."

"Really? I didn't know you wrote poetry. You are supposed to be my best friend! What else are you keeping from me?"

AJ cracks a smile and says, "I've been writing for years, but I'm not that good. It's just for my own comfort."

"I'll be the judge of how good you are. When can I read some of your work?"

"*Never!*" AJ shakes his head. "Naw, I'm just playing. I'll let you read one when we go back to my house."

"What type of poems do you write?"

"It all depends on what I'm feeling at the time. I have some about faith, love, relationships, family, birds, giving up, life—but lately, they have all been about domestic violence. Which one would you like to read? If I was to let you, that is."

"What do you mean, if you was to let me? Sir, you are going to let me," Connie says with a big smile.

"Okay, okay, I'll let you."

"Thought so!" Connie laughs. "Boy, I was about to pull this car over and let you have it."

"Naw, don't do that. For a lil' woman, your punches hurt."

"Okay, AJ, we are back at your house, so go get them."

"Go get what?"

"Oh, so we playin' dumb now?"

"Naw, just playing. I'll get them. Which ones do you want to read first?"

"Just bring them *all*!"

"Okay, you don't have to be mean." As AJ enters the house, he notices his mom's bedroom light is still on, so he knocks on her door to let her know he's back. He calls out, "Are you okay, Mom?"

"Yes, I am," she replies. "Are you okay?"

"Yes ma'am. I'll be outside with Connie if you need me." He turns and picks up his backpack and heads back outside, announcing his presence to Connie as she waits in the car with the windows rolled down. "I'm back! Are you sure you want to read these? They are not very good." He opens the passenger door.

"Boy, just give them to me."

"Here, read this one first." As he hands her the first poem, he closes the car door and waits outside.

"What are you doing?" Connie shouts at him through the open window. "Why are you standing out there?"

"I'm not good at listening to other people read what I write, so I kind of distance myself till they are finished."

"Get your butt in here!"

As AJ reopens the door, Connie begins to read . . .

When You Say "I Love You"—What Did I Miss?

> *Why is it when you say "I love you,"*
> *It's after your hand has come down on me?*
> *Why is it when you say "I love you,"*
> *It's after blood is pouring?*
> *Why is it when you say "I love you,"*
> *It's after the cops arrive?*
> *What am I missing . . . ?*
>
> *In the beginning, when you said "I love you,"*
> *It was before a kiss.*
> *In the beginning, when you said "I love you,"*
> *It was while holding me.*
> *In the beginning, when you said "I love you,"*
> *It was during a night of romance.*
> *What am I missing . . . ?*

Connie pauses for a short moment and glances over at AJ, then continues reading.

> *Why is it when you say "I love you,"*
> *It's after my tears are flowing?*
> *Why is it when you say "I love you,"*
> *It's after my ribs are broken?*

Why is it when you say "I love you,"

It's after I've been laid in my grave?

Why is it when you say "I love you,"

It's after you place a rose at my headstone?

What did I miss . . . ?

With tears in her eyes, she looks over at AJ again, and for a moment all she can say is "Wow."

"Don't start that crying stuff! You know I'm not with that." AJ ducks his head to avoid her eye contact.

"This poem is very moving. Anyone who reads this will cry—it's heartfelt and written through the eyes of a battered woman. It's obvious that you understand the pain, suffering, and heartache that battered women face. So why don't you do something with this?"

"I told you—it's only how I cope with what's going on in my life."

"But, AJ, there are so many women whose realities *are* this poem! Please use this to show people that domestic violence is a problem in many homes. Maybe—just maybe—someone who is experiencing this will realize that this could be them and seek help."

AJ smirks and says, "Fat chance."

"Why do you say that?"

"Remember, I've seen it firsthand, and these women know they need help, like my mom, but they are too afraid to talk to someone or even ask for help."

"Sounds like someone I know," states Connie.

"I'm not afraid. I just don't want people in my business."

"I'm going to remember that when someone dies."

"Will you just read the next one already?"

"Which one do you want me to read next?"

AJ flips through his folder. "Here's one. It's also about domestic violence. Don't start that crying stuff again, though."

"No promises," Connie says.

"It's called 'A Thousand Sorries.'"

"Will you just give it to me already?"

A Thousand Sorries

When we first met, I told you that

I'd been hurt.

You said from your lips

Would only come respect.

A thousand sorries later,

Meeting you I regret . . .

You said you would never

Raise your hand to me.

A thousand sorries later,

You can still see where my lip was split . . .

You told me you loved me

And would protect me.

A thousand sorries later,

I need protection from you . . .

In the beginning you said
I was your world.
A thousand sorries later,
My world has ended . . .

A thousand sorries have taken me
From the people I love.
A thousand sorries later,
I am no more.

With tears forming in her eyes, again Connie states, "AJ, these are beautiful and sad at the same time. You should do something with them, like get them published."

"That will never happen." AJ shakes his head.

"Why would you say that?"

"Because, Connie, people know things like this go on, but nobody wants to read about it, especially if it's in a poem."

"I bet if your favorite poet was still alive, she would tell you what I'm telling you."

"Girl, please. Maya Angelou wouldn't read my poems."

"And why not?"

"'Cause I'm nowhere near her realm of poetry. Besides, this is just for me."

"Your poetry speaks the truth of what could be the reality for hundreds of women, and if you can give them a voice to be heard—even if it's through poetry—people would listen."

"Yeah, right!"

"Promise me you will at least think about it."

AJ replies, "Yeah, I promise," with a sarcastic tone in his voice.

"I'm serious, AJ. Think about it. Maybe—just maybe—this could be the perfect way to get your mom and dad to listen to how you feel about your family's problems. If you don't do something with them, I will."

"Okay, I'll think about it. It's getting late. Shouldn't you be getting back to your house?"

"Yeah, I guess so, and you need to go in and talk to your mom."

"Well . . . it's not *that* late!"

Connie shakes her head. "Boy, get your butt in there, and talk to your mom."

As Connie ushers him out of the car, AJ says, "Thanks for listening to my problems."

"That's what real friends do," Connie replies. "I want to read more of your poems when I come by tomorrow, okay?"

"Sure. Good night." As AJ enters the house, he notices this time that his mom's bedroom light is off. He thinks to himself, "Thank God she's asleep, 'cause I don't want to talk about that man tonight." He walks to his room and begins to think about Connie's suggestion. "Maybe I *should* talk to someone, 'cause if I don't, I might lose it next time."

As AJ gets ready for bed, his phone rings.

"Hello, hello," he answers.

"Hey, AJ. It's me, Connie. I just wanted to call and let you know I made it home."

"I figured you had. You live two blocks away, you know."

"Ha ha, don't try to be funny," states Connie.

"Hey, Connie, I was thinking—you are right. I do need to talk to someone."

"Good. So are you going to talk to Ms. Allie on Monday when we get back to school?"

"Let me sleep on it, and I'll let you know tomorrow."

"I'll be over after I pick my mom up."

"Girl, don't she get off at like nine?"

"Yeah. And?"

"I can tell you now I'm not gonna be up that early."

"You better be, and you better have me some waffles ready." Connie laughs. "And don't burn them this time!"

"When did we get married? Let me know, 'cause only my wife would get away with talking to me like that," AJ states, trying to hold in his own laughter.

"I'm the next best thing—I'm your best friend. Now take your butt to bed so you can get my breakfast ready in the morning. Good night."

Before AJ goes to bed, he sits down at his computer and looks up websites where he could submit his poetry. As he looks through all the websites, he is quickly overwhelmed by all the poems he sees that contain sadness and despair.

"This is going to be tougher than I thought. Which site is the best for my type of poetry?" he wonders to himself. "Oh well. I'll deal with it tomorrow. I'm going to bed."

CHAPTER TWO

THE HARRISES' HOUSE

THE NEXT DAY

Early the next morning, here comes Connie, knocking on the Harrises' front door. AJ's mom answers it.

"Hi, Mrs. Harris. Is AJ up?"

"You must be Connie. Come on in. He's in the kitchen making breakfast, which he rarely does, but I can see why he is now. Let me get him for you." Mrs. Harris disappears into the kitchen while Connie waits. She can hear Mrs. Harris say, "Anthony, there's a very lovely young lady in the living room for you."

"Mom, she's just a friend. That's all."

"I wish my friends made me breakfast," his mom states with a playful tone.

"It's not like that, for real."

"Okay. Well, I'm headed out for a while. I'll be back around four. You kids have a good time."

"Okay. Bye, Mom," AJ says.

As AJ's mom leaves, she tells Connie, "It was nice to meet you. You can go in the kitchen if you want."

"Yes ma'am. Nice to meet you as well." Connie joins AJ in the kitchen. "AJ, your mom seems nice."

"She is when *he* is not here."

"Do you ever call him your dad, or do you just refer to him as *that man* or *him*?"

"Not recently, I don't. Like I said last night—he's just a sperm donor."

"Okay." Connie drops the subject. "Breakfast smells good, by the way. What all are you making?"

"Well, I didn't want to just make waffles, so I cooked up some egg whites into a nice veggie omelet, along with whole-grain waffles topped with strawberries and blueberries and a bit of powdered sugar, turkey bacon, and, of course, fresh orange juice."

"Wow, look at you trying to be a lil' chef." Connie laughs teasingly.

"Well, you know I can get down in the kitchen when I want to."

"Sounds like it. But honestly, how much did you burn before I got here?"

"*None*, thank you very much," AJ insists.

"Well, I want to read some more of your poems while I eat my breakfast."

"Okay, but I'm not giving you no sad ones. I don't want any tears in my food, you crybaby."

"It's your fault!"

"I'll go get them."

Connie sits down at the counter overlooking the pool and waits for AJ to return to fix her a plate. Upon his return with his folder in hand, he asks, "You're not hungry?"

"Yes, I am, but I was waiting on you."

"I cooked, so you have to fix your own plate."

"Seriously?"

"Yes, seriously. I'm a chef, not a waiter, remember?" AJ says with a smile as he hands her an empty plate. They begin to pile food on their plates.

"You mean you *try* to be a chef," Connie says sarcastically.

"Are you gonna eat or just talk smack?"

"I'mma do both. Now what?"

"Well, I guess I'll keep my poems to myself." He sets his plate on the counter and begins to eat, pretending to be disinterested in her.

"If you do, you see this fork? I'mma stick it right in your—"

AJ hastily interrupts her, "All right, all right. Here you go. Such a drama queen."

"Yes, I am. So what?"

AJ shifts the subject back to the poems. "Since you brought up Maya Angelou last night, I wrote one for her. Here, read it."

Connie reaches for the poem and, at the same time, says, "These waffles are really good. I guess you do know what you are doing sometimes."

"Still talking smack, I see."

"Yep, and I'm gonna keep it up."

"Girl, just read the poem already."

"Don't rush me." Connie begins to read the title and says, "So far, good title."

Threshold of Hope

Through the pain, I survive,
With your words of wisdom
Running through my mind . . .

Changes have come over the years,
Yet I am still me . . .

Your words echo through my soul
And explode from within my pen.
You are my threshold of hope . . .

Today I must mourn,
For a blessed angel
has been called home . . .

Just to hear your name
Fills me with grace.
I will continue my writings
Because of you . . .

Maya Angelou,
You are my threshold of hope . . .

"Seriously, Connie, are you tearing up again?"

"I'm sorry! I can't help it. The way you write has so much feeling in it, from start to finish."

"Do you want more food, or are you done eating?"

"Why are you trying to change the subject?"

"I'm not. I'm just asking 'cause I'm full already."

"Naw, I'm good. Save some for your mom. Where did she go, anyway?"

"I'm not sure, but I think she went to the jail to see him."

"Did you talk with her?"

"Nope. When I made it in last night, she was asleep."

"Well, you need to."

"I will. I don't want to, but if it helps her, I will. Okay, now I'm changing the subject. Last night, I wanted to upload one of my poems to a website, but there are so many different sites. I didn't know which one was the best one to get my poems read."

"There are a few I would use, like the Poetry Society of America, or you can get this app called Wattpad and upload your poems and get reviews on them."

"Will you help me with that?"

"Sure. You know Chris from school? He has Wattpad, and he's gotten over two hundred people following his page."

"Oh, yeah, that sounds like something I might do."

"It would be good for you to get them out there so others can read them."

"Maybe you're right."

"Maybe? No, I am right. I'm always right."

"Sure, if you say so, Connie." AJ shakes his head with a small smile on his face.

"Anyway, what made you write the one about Maya Angelou?"

"Well, she is my favorite poet, and when I read her poems, they lift me up from dark places. She's part of the reason why I began writing in the first place."

"If reading her poems made you able to write like you do, she was a very good teacher."

"I wish I could have met her before she passed." AJ sighs.

"I think she would have loved to meet you too." Connie turns at a sound from the driveway. "Hey, I think your mom is pulling back up."

"Naw, she said she will be home about four."

Connie peers through the blinds covering the window. "Well, someone is pulling up in a taxi."

AJ gets up and looks out the window as a man steps out of the car. "Oh shit, it's him!"

"*Him* who?" Connie asks.

"It's my dad! What the hell is he doing out so soon?" AJ nearly shouts.

"Should I be leaving?"

"No, you don't have to go anywhere."

AJ's dad stumbles to the door. AJ shakes his head. "Look at him—he's still drunk, and he can barely walk."

"Shouldn't you go help him?"

"Hell no. I hope he falls on his ass."

"You shouldn't say things like that. Don't be like him."

"Oh, trust me—I'm nothing like him."

There's a pounding on the door as AJ's dad yells, "Janice, open this damn door before I kick it in!"

Connie edges toward the back door. "AJ, I think I better leave. Your dad sounds crazy."

"Hold on—I'll go let him in. Just stay here, okay?"

Connie watches through the window. By the time AJ makes it to the door, his mother is pulling up to the house. As Mrs. Harris gets out, Anthony Sr. turns and says, "Where the hell you been, dressed all up like that, huh?"

"I went to pay your bail but was told you was released because the bartender didn't press charges."

Anthony Sr. reaches for Mrs. Harris's arm, but she quickly pulls back.

She snaps, "You stink! You smell like you drank the whole damn bar."

He then snatches her by the arm and says, "Who you talking to like that, woman? Don't you know I'll just—"

AJ opens the door and pushes his dad away from his mother.

His father glares at him. "Oh, you a man now? You want to buck up at me? Well, let's go."

AJ's mom grabs him and tells him to go back inside.

"No, Mom! 'Cause if he touches you again, I will kill him."

His father scoffs. "Oh, oh, oh—so you that big and bad, you gonna kill me?"

"Touch her again, and I will. Why don't you take your drunk ass on somewhere else? We don't need you here."

Connie steps outside and tells AJ, "Please come back in."

"Who the fuck is that? Now I see why you acting big—'cause you got your lil' girlfriend over. Ha, boy, if your mama and that lil' bi—" Before Anthony Sr. can finish, AJ pushes past his mother and pops his dad square in the mouth.

Connie and Mrs. Harris grab AJ and force him down the driveway to Connie's car. Mrs. Harris begs Connie, "Please take him somewhere before someone calls the police."

Anthony Sr. recovers, wiping the blood from his mouth, and yells out, "Boy, you hit like a lil' bitch!" He stumbles into the house.

Connie and AJ back out the driveway, and his mother follows suit.

***

While driving with no real destination in mind, Janice thinks to herself, "It's time to leave. My son doesn't need this in his life, and neither do I." She grips the steering wheel with her shaky hands.

Janice drives until she finds herself at an old friend's house.

Her friend Darlene answers her knock at the front door. "Hey, Jan. Come on in, girl. How have you been?"

"Not so good," Janice admits. "My husband's gone off the deep end with his drinking, to the point I can't stand it."

"Girl, you need to get out of that situation before it gets worse!" Darlene leads the way into her living room.

"It can't get any worse." Janice plops down onto a sofa and buries her face in her hands.

"It can if he kills you."

"I'm sorry to put this on you, but I had no one else to turn to."

"Hey, what's a friend for if not to help?" Darlene joins Janice on the couch.

"Thank you. He got out of jail today because yesterday he got drunk and tore up a bar. The bartender didn't press charges, though I wish he had, 'cause when Anthony made it home, he was still drunk and was about to jump on me. Thank God my son was there. That look he had—I was sure he would have killed me."

"Jan, you can't go back to that house, or next time he just might."

"I know, but where else can I go?"

"Honey, listen to me." Darlene places a hand on Janice's shoulder. "Kevin has gone off to college. You can stay in his room, and Anthony Jr. can stay in the game room till he leaves for college."

"I don't want to intrude on your space."

"Trust me—you're not. Besides, I would love the company. With Kevin gone, it's a little too quiet around here."

"I have to go back over there at some point to get my things."

"Don't go over there alone, but if you have to, take my gun in case he tries something."

Janice hesitates, then insists, "You know I don't like guns. I'll just have the police go with me."

"Yeah, that is a better option, 'cause you don't want attempted murder on your hands."

"Oh, it wouldn't be *attempted* murder . . ." Janice looks at her friend and can't contain herself any longer. "Darlene, I'm not being fully honest with you. I haven't told anyone yet, but I . . . I got myself a gun, permit and everything, not too long ago. I've prayed to God that I wouldn't have to use it, but with the way things have been escalating, I worried that I might have to protect myself one of these days."

Darlene is quick to place a gentle hand on her friend's arm, reassuring her that there is no judgement for keeping this a secret. "How long has this been going on?"

Janice looks down at her trembling hands. "It's been a few years, but he always says he's sorry, and for a few weeks after, he is the sweetest man I ever met."

"Baby girl, I'mma tell you like my mama used to say, and remember this. Anybody can say *I'm sorry*, but a man—a real man who truly loves you—would never have to say he's sorry for hitting you, 'cause a real man knows the only touching that his hand should do to a woman is to hold her, and the only actions he should show you is how much he loves you. If he's doing anything other than that, don't say he's the sweetest man you ever met, because hitting you is nothing sweet, and he for sure isn't a man."

"I know all of what you are saying, but—"

"No buts, Janice," Darlene says adamantly. "If that man truly loves you, there is no way he would hit you. There are a thousand women that say they want a good man but always end up with the thugs that beat on them. No woman deserves that! Over half those women can't get help 'cause they stay with abusive men, and the men end up killing them. Now you have the chance, baby. Find a way to get some help. Don't be one of those women who ask God to save them right before they die. Be the woman who says, 'I'm still here because God provided me with the strength to walk away.' I'm telling you this because I love you like my lil' sister, and I only want the best for you and your son. Speaking of your son, where is he?"

"Oh, he's with his friend. After he punched his dad in the mouth, I had his friend take him away before they really started fighting."

"Sounds like he had it coming. Janice, I have something I want to give you. Any time you feel in despair, please read it. It has been a great help to me and has healed all the pain that has come my way."

"What is it?"

"It's a poem by someone you know very well. It's a poem called 'Salvation.' Here, read it, but don't read who it's by till the end."

Salvation

I seem to have lost my way.

This path looks unfamiliar to me.

It's leading me into darkness,

A place I don't feel safe.

This house I lie in is not my home.

This place I feel I don't belong . . .

I seem to have lost my way.

I look around and don't know

Where I am.

I try to keep my feet on solid ground,

Yet my mind flies away.

I continue hoping to find my way back.

The farther I go, the stronger I feel . . .

I seem to have lost my way.

I fall to my knees and pray.

Father God, please help me find

My way back to you . . .

I hear a voice call out,

"My daughter, follow me."

Salvation is near . . .

—Anthony Harris

With tears in her eyes, Janice looks over at her friend and says, "Darlene, when did my son write this?"

"Remember when my husband died? I didn't know what to do or who to turn to at the funeral, but he gave this to me, and I've carried it ever since."

"I didn't know he was even interested in poetry."

"I have another one that he gave me a few days later."

"Can I please read it?" Janice wipes away a lone tear.

"Sure, let me go get it. I framed it and put it over my bed. It's a prayer that I say every night."

Janice places her hand over her mouth and thinks about how much that poem she read seems to reflect how she feels every day. Darlene returns with a beautiful framed poem.

"Here you go. I hope you love it as much as I do."

This I Pray

Take my hand and guide me

Unto your salvation.

Leadeth me to your mountaintop.

Show me the way of your word.

Take my pain and remove all that hurts.

Give unto me the joy that hides within.

Watch my steps and help them

To remain on the path that your son

Has carved for me.

Give unto me the strength

To lead all who are tempted

To fall beneath this earth.

Lord, hear my prayer and

Strengthen my faith, that

An angel with broken wings

Will once again fly to the heavens.

This I pray, Amen . . .

—Anthony Harris

"Wow," states Janice, again wiping tears from her cheeks. "How am I so wrapped up in my own world that I didn't know my son could write like this?"

"Baby, I think he understands that you have a lot to deal with at home. Before Kevin left, I heard the boys talking, and he said that he had left one of his poems lying in the house in hopes that you would read it, but your husband came in mad about something, and you'd set it down. Anthony figured that you wouldn't go back to it, so he put it up."

"I remember finding his tablet in an odd spot recently, but I thought it was just schoolwork. Now I wish I had read it."

"I'm sure if you just ask him, he would allow you to read them. I think he would actually like that you are interested in his writing. You should call him and talk. Y'all have a lot to talk about."

"You're right. I'm about to call him."

"Okay, I'll leave you two to talk. I'm gonna make a run to the store."

Janice picks up the phone and calls AJ but gets his voice mail instead of him. She waits a few moments and tries again. This time he picks up.

"Hey, Mom. Sorry I didn't pick up when you called the first time."

"That's okay, son. Where are you?"

"We are at Grandy's, grabbing a bite to eat but about to head back to the house."

"Don't go back there!"

"Wait, huh? Mom, where are you?"

"I'm at Darlene's. I'm not going back to that house either."

"Okay, Mom. I'll get Connie to bring me over there instead."

"Alright, son. I'll see you when you get here."

***

"What's wrong?" Connie asks as she and AJ, full from Grandy's, slide back into her car.

"I think my mom is finally leaving him."

"Where is she?"

"She's at her friend's house. I call her friend my aunt 'cause they've been friends for years. If you don't mind, could you take me over there? It's not too far from here."

"Of course I will—you know that."

"Thanks, Connie. I don't know what I would do without you."

"You'd go crazier than you already are."

"I see you still got jokes."

"Yep, all day. What are you gonna do about it?"

"You know I'm not scared of your lil' short self, right?"

"You will be if I stop this car."

"Alright, lil' bit, just keep driving, and I'll keep quiet."

"Thought so," Connie states with a stern voice.

"Will you just drive? It's just a few more blocks."

Connie can't stay silent for long. "So are you gonna talk to your mom about your dad?"

"I think that's what she wants to talk about. She said she's not going back to the house, so I'm guessing she has reached her point of no return." He points up ahead. "There's her car. You can let me out here. Thanks again, Connie."

"No problem, AJ. Just be careful, and take care of your mother, okay?"

"I will, and you be careful going home. Call me when you get home."

"I will. Bye, Ant."

"Bye, Connie. See you at school tomorrow."

"Okay, call me if you need a ride."

"Will do, Connie."

AJ approaches Darlene's door. As he nears, his mother opens the door and hugs him tightly.

"Mom, are you okay?"

"Yes, I am. I just wanted to show you that I love you, and I am so proud of you."

"You are proud of me for punching Dad?"

"No, boy, I'm proud of you because you are the best part of me, and Darlene let me read some of your poetry. She also told me that she overheard you telling Kevin you left some of your poems lying around for me to read. Baby, I'm sorry I didn't pay closer attention to what you were doing, but I would love to read them."

"Okay, Mom, but first, could you loosen up? You're choking me."

"Oh, sorry, baby."

"Mom, are you sure you want to read them? They are about domestic violence."

"Yes, I am sure."

"Okay, I have a few of them in my backpack. They are pretty sad, though."

"Guess I better get some tissues."

"Aw, Mom, don't tell me you have teary eyes too."

His mom begins to read "When You Say 'I Love You,'" and soon after, her eyes start to form tears.

"This poem is beautiful and heartfelt, Anthony. Is this how you saw my life going?"

"I'm sorry, Mom, but yes. It's not just your life, but the life of any woman who is in a situation that could end their life by someone who claims they love them. After seeing how Dad treats you, and after seeing you try to cover the bruises, I felt the only thing I could do was to write about it, and hopefully you would see it and realize that you need to seek help. Again, Mom, I'm sorry."

"Son, you don't have anything to be sorry about. I should have never let it get this far. I should have protected you from this, but I am going to do something about it now."

"What are you talking about, Mom? What are you going to do?"

"I'm leaving your father. I can't keep going through this. Darlene said we could stay here for a while, but if you want to go home, we can."

"Mom, I don't want you getting hurt anymore. If that means we have to be somewhere else other than home, then I'm okay with it."

"That's good, 'cause I am not going back there for as long as he refuses to get help. There was a time your dad was a sweet and caring man. You actually have a part of him that I miss. He used to write poetry when we first met. I carry with me every day the first poem he wrote for me in college, as a reminder of the man I fell in love with."

"Wow, I can't believe he wrote poetry—based on how he is now, that is."

"He wanted to turn it into a song for someone like Carrie Underwood or John Legend to sing, but I wanted it to stay just as it is."

"Could I read it sometime?"

"Sure, whenever you want to."

"Well, Mom, I'm going to head to bed. Gotta be ready for school in the morning. Love you, Mom."

"Love you too, son. Good night." She gives him another quick hug, and then he steps away.

He stops in the doorway and turns back to his mom. "Oh, you don't have to take me to school tomorrow. I'm gonna have Connie pick me up. And, Mom, can I take that poem with me? I want Connie to see it."

***

Darlene returns home and asks Janice if she talked to AJ about her decision not to return home. Janice states that she did and that she also talked to him about his poetry.

"He let me read one that he wrote, which pretty much was about the direction he felt my life was headed if I stayed with his father."

"What did you think about the poem?"

"Well, you know, I cried after I read it," Janice admits. "It was truly sad and a very strong message about what could happen if I were to stay. It seems that all his poems have deep meanings that a lot of people could relate to."

"Yeah. I cried, too, when I read the one he gave me," Darlene replies.

CHAPTER THREE

DARLENE'S HOME

THE NEXT MORNING

The next morning, as AJ gets ready for school, he calls Connie to pick him up. They talk as she heads out the door to pick him up, and he tells her that he has a poem that he would like her to read.

"Truth is, though, it's a poem by my dad," he tells her.

Connie pauses, then says, "Wait, that mean drunk writes poetry?"

"Yeah, it was a surprise to me too. He also wanted someone like Carrie Underwood or John Legend to turn it into a song," AJ repeats what his mom told him.

"Wow, it must be pretty good. Have you read it?"

"Naw, I wanted you to read it first. My mom says it's the first one he ever wrote her, and she keeps it to remind herself of the man he was when they got married." AJ shifts the subject abruptly. "When you pick me up, do you mind running me by the house to pick up a few things before school?"

"Thought you said your mom told you not to go back over there without her?"

"Yeah, she did, but I have to get some papers for school. Plus I need to get some of my clothes."

Connie hesitates, then responds, "Okay . . . but just know I'm totally against it."

"I'll only be a few minutes. I promise."

"I'm about to pull up, so come on out. Don't keep me waiting."

"I just gotta put my shoes on, and I'll be ready." He pulls on the shoes he wore yesterday. Earlier this morning, Darlene was able to scrounge together an outfit from Kevin's clothes that he'd left behind when he went off for college.

"AJ, don't forget the poem."

"I won't," AJ insists. "I'm on my way down." He tromps down the stairs.

After a brief silence on the line, Connie says, "On my way past your house, I saw your dad sitting on the porch, already drinking this early in the morning."

"Are you sure, Con? He should be on his way to work."

"I'm very sure. Do you still want to stop by there?"

AJ sighs and considers the consequences of running into his dad again. "With him there, not really, but I do need those papers."

"What are they for, AJ?"

"They are some college applications I need to turn in today."

"So you decided to go ahead and give college a shot?"

"My mom decided for me. Ha." AJ laughs.

"Told you she wouldn't let you mess up your future. Are you on your way out?"

"Yes, yes. I'm just making a sandwich for lunch." AJ balances the phone between his cheek and shoulder as he hurries to throw together a decent sandwich with the supplies his mom left on the counter for him.

"Well, hurry up. The meter is ticking."

"Oh, it's like that now?"

"Yepper. If I gotta sit and wait, you gotta pay."

"I'mma remember that."

"Remember it, write it down, take a picture—I don't give a fuck."

"This is not *Friday*, and you are not Chris Tucker." AJ shakes his head as he stuffs his sandwich into a plastic bag.

"No, but I'mma be Deebo and knock you the fuck out if you don't hurry up."

"Okay, okay. I'm heading out the door now."

As AJ opens the car door, Connie states, "Bet you forgot the poem."

"Nope!" AJ replies. "Got it right here."

Connie reaches her hand over demandingly. "Well, give it to me."

"Can I get in the car first?"

"I'm not stopping you, slowpoke." She smiles playfully.

"Here." AJ pulls the poem out of his bag and shoves it into Connie's outstretched hand before sliding into the passenger seat. "It's called 'I Wanna Make Love to You.'"

"I can read the title myself, you know."

As Connie starts to read, AJ interrupts, "You gonna read it *now*?"

"Yes, I am. Got a problem with that?"

"Yeah, just one . . ."

"Which is . . . ?"

"Is the meter still running?" AJ smirks.

Connie rolls her eyes. "Boy, just sit there and shut up. You can't rush perfection."

"Oh, but *you* can?"

"When did I do that?"

"When you was rushing me to come out." AJ folds his arms.

"Oh, well, that's different." Connie waves her hand at him and tries to return her attention to the poem.

"Why is that?"

"'Cause you're not perfect like me. Now be quiet so I can read."

I Want to Make Love to You

> I want to make love to you.
>
> I want to feel your most intimate thoughts.
>
> I want to touch your deepest feelings . . .
>
>
> Let me tease you with
> my fingertips.
> Let me kiss you gently
> on your lips.
> Let me feel your breath

as the intense passion

becomes overwhelming.

Let me entwine my heart

with yours . . .

I want to make love to you.

I want to feel your most intimate thoughts.

I want to touch your deepest feelings . . .

Allow me to caress your

silky skin.

Allow me to stare deep

into your eyes.

As if they were the window

to your soul.

Allow me to take your hand

And follow you to your

Secret place of abundant

Life, pleasure, and pain . . .

I want to make love to you

From the deepest parts of your soul,

To the warmest parts of your heart,

From the strongest of your touch,

To the softest of your kiss . . .

Baby, I just want to make love to

you . . .

"Oh my God," Connie states with a look of shock plastered on her face.

"What's wrong, Con?" AJ asks, still in the dark about the contents of the poem. "Is it that bad?"

"No, it's that *good*. I can see why your mom fell in love with him then. What I *can't* see is how he went from this to being the way he is now? After reading this, I can tell you that the best part of your dad made its way into your DNA."

"Thanks, I guess," AJ replies. "You know, sometimes I wish he would just admit he has a problem and get help, but I know that's not going to happen."

"I'm sure once he sees that your mom is serious, he'll realize he needs help."

"Yeah, right," AJ sarcastically answers, turning his gaze out the window. "Okay, let's go before school starts, or do you need some time to wipe away the tears again, Con?"

"I'm not crying this time, for your information," Connie responds.

"Then why are we still sitting here?"

"'Cause I want to. You got a problem with that?"

"Is that your favorite saying? 'Cause I think you say that so you can have a reason to punch me."

"Boy, hush. If I wanted to hit you, I just would." Connie laughs. "Anyway, we are about to leave." She starts up the car.

"Don't forget to stop by the house for me, okay?"

"Yeah, yeah, yeah, I know—you need to get some papers. But what are you going to do if he is still there drinking?"

"We are just going to get some papers and some clothes, so I'm not going to do anything but that."

"Promise?"

AJ sighs. "Yes, Con, I promise."

"Well then, let's go before school starts."

"That's what I've been trying to tell you."

"Do you want to walk? If not, just sit there and be quiet."

"You do realize I'm older than you?"

"So? And do you realize you are in my car?"

AJ laughs. "All right, you got this one."

"Correction—I got them all."

"One of these days I will get a win over you."

"Yeah, when I let you."

"Just drive, Ms. Smarty-Pants."

As AJ and Connie drive toward his house, she asks if he has plans for what to do with his poetry.

He shrugs. "I don't know what to do."

"Well, maybe we can figure it out together," she offers.

"I'd like that as long as I feel comfortable with the ideas you come up with."

As they turn down the street AJ lives on, they can see his father still sitting out on the porch, drinking away. As they draw closer, Connie again asks AJ if he is sure he wants to stop. He assures her he does, so they continue on into the driveway. Before they can even stop, AJ's dad is already yelling.

"What the hell you want?" his dad yells.

AJ in return responds in a calm voice, "I didn't come to fight or argue with you. I just need to get some things for school." He steps toward the house and shuts the car door behind him.

"Naw, remember—you big and bad! I guess you not as bad as you thought when no one is around."

"Man, I did what I did to protect my mom from you. I wasn't gonna stand there and let you hit her again. Will you just move and let me get my things?" AJ stands his ground.

"Sure, go right ahead."

As AJ proceeds to go inside, his dad sucker punches him in the back of the head, knocking him into the house and onto the floor. Connie jumps out the car and runs to try and help her friend, but AJ's dad closes the front door before she can get there. As she beats on the door, AJ yells at his dad, "What the fuck is wrong with you?"

His dad answers back, "That was for yesterday, you lil' punk! Now get up, and let's see how bad you really are."

AJ sees one of his dad's golf clubs and grabs it. In a flash, his dad slaps him across his face.

"What you gonna do with that club besides make me mad?"

"I don't want to fight you. I just want to get my things and go to school."

Connie is still banging on the door and screaming, "I'm about to call the police!" As she starts down the driveway to her car to get her phone, the front door swings open, and AJ backs out with the golf club raised as if he is ready to swing.

Connie runs back to him, yelling, "AJ, are you okay?"

He closes the front door and turns toward her. "Yeah, I'm all right," he mutters.

"No, you are not! Your lip is bleeding! I'm calling the police." She turns swiftly to retrieve her cell phone.

"*Don't!*" AJ insists. "Let's just go to school. Trust me—I'm okay."

"What are you going to say if anyone asks what happened?"

"I'm not sure, but I'll think of something." AJ walks to the car and slides into the passenger seat, holding his backpack in his lap.

"You need to go to the nurse and get that knot looked at."

"Don't worry. I will."

Connie finally relents and joins him in the car.

As she drives them to school, Connie notices AJ starting to nod off.

"Are you sure you are going to be okay?"

"Yes, I am." He leans his head against the window. "Will you stop worrying? It's just a lil' bump."

"Well, I can't. You seem to be spacing out."

"No, I'm just in deep thought."

"Sure, you are," Connie sarcastically states, gripping the steering wheel in aggravation. "Will you promise me that you will get checked out when we get to school?"

"Will that make you feel better if I do?"

"You know it will."

"Okay, I'll get it checked out as soon as we get there."

"And call your mom!"

AJ shakes his head quickly. "Oh, hell no! She will go kill that man!"

"Someone needs to do something to him to set him straight."

"Don't worry. He will get all that he deserves on judgement day."

Connie puts the car in park. "We are here. Now go straight to the nurse's office before class starts. I have to go to band practice, so I will see you after, okay?"

"Yes, Mama, I'm going!"

"Oh, we got jokes? Don't make me lump up the other side of your head."

"Why you always talking about hitting me? You so violent." AJ throws the car door open and steps out. Connie follows suit.

"Boy, hush, and get your butt to that office."

"See, you sound just like my mom."

As AJ heads off to the nurse's office, he looks back at Connie and smiles, thinking about how lucky he is to have someone in his life who cares for him the way she does.

The farther he walks, the dizzier he gets. He drops down on a bench to wait out the dizziness, but he soon realizes he is not only dizzy, but his vision is also getting very blurry. Something is not right. AJ attempts to call Connie, but his trembling hands fail to get the job done before his vision completely slips to black.

***

After band practice, Connie notices a crowd and paramedics gathered near the senior lunch benches. She rushes over to see what's happening. As she gets closer, she's stopped by one of her bandmates, who tells her the paramedics are here for AJ. The girl tells Connie that she was the first to find him passed out on the ground. She tried to call Connie, but Connie didn't hear her phone ring during band practice. Upon hearing the news, Connie quickly runs back to the band room and grabs her things to contact AJ's mom and let her know what is going on. Just before she can place the call, she hears her name being called over the school's PA system. She's being asked to come to the principal's office. She hurriedly makes her way to the office while nervously trying to dial AJ's mom. She has her cell phone number saved in her phone in case of emergencies—just for times like now.

As she reaches for the office door, she is met by Ms. Allie, the school counselor.

"Connie, could I speak with you about Anthony?" Ms. Allie asks in a gentle tone.

"Yes ma'am. Is he okay? I need to call his mom."

"Don't worry about that—she has already been notified. Do you know what happened to Anthony and how he got that knot on the back of his head? Before he left in the ambulance, he said he got jumped by some guys this morning. I know you two are always together, and somehow I don't think that's what happened."

"Ms. Allie, I was with him this morning, and he didn't get jumped. But I promised him I wouldn't say anything."

"Connie, I understand you made a promise, but if Anthony is in any kind of trouble, that's one promise I don't think you should keep. He could have been seriously hurt. He is okay this time, but what about next time?"

"He's not in any trouble with anyone, Ms. Allie. I promise."

"Then how did he get that knot on the back of his head and the bruise on his face?"

"Ms. Allie, I'm sorry, but I promised. If there is nothing else, Ms. Allie, I need to go to the hospital and check on AJ."

"Okay, go ahead, but we are not done talking about this. Just remember—next time it could be more than a knot on the head.

Talk with him, and try to convince him to talk to someone. If not me, then someone else. Please."

"Yes ma'am. I will."

Connie scurries out of the office and bolts to her car with the intention of heading straight toward the hospital, but just as she reaches the parking lot, she is stopped again. Only this time, it's by school police.

"Ms. Smalls, may I speak with you before you leave?"

"I'm in a bit of a rush." Connie bounces back and forth on her feet, impatient to have this conversation over with so she can go see AJ.

"I understand that, and I won't keep you long. I just need to speak with you about what occurred this morning with Anthony Harris and how he was injured. I have spoken with several students, and they all assured me if anyone knew what happened, you are who I need to speak with."

"I don't have anything to say now. If you don't mind, may I go now?"

The officer places both hands on his hips. "Ms. Smalls, this is a very serious matter, and I intend on finding out who caused this and how it happened."

"AJ is my friend, but will you please leave me out of it?"

"If he truly is your friend, wouldn't you do everything possible to help him?"

Connie turns toward her car, and with tears forming in her eyes, she says, "You don't understand. I want to say what happened, but I promised him I wouldn't say anything."

"Some promises are meant to be broken when harm comes to those we love, and I can tell you love him, maybe even more than you or he even knows."

Without saying another word, Connie runs to her car. The tears spill before she can even pull out of the parking lot.

When Connie arrives at the hospital, she sees AJ's mom standing outside, smoking and looking around as if she is waiting on someone.

Connie parks quickly and runs up to AJ's mom. "Mrs. Harris, is AJ okay? What did the doctors say?"

"He is okay, but he has a mild concussion. His dad is coming to pick us up."

"No, Mrs. Harris, he can't!" Connie's jaw hangs open as she is astonished by the very idea.

"Calm down, Connie."

"Mrs. Harris, he is the reason AJ is here."

Janice's tired eyes meet Connie's earnest gaze. "What are you talking about? AJ fell down and hit his head at school."

"No, he didn't! His dad did this to him this morning before school!"

"Connie, are you telling me his dad beat him up?"

"I promised I wouldn't say anything, but yes." Connie clasps her hands together to convey her genuine concern.

"Please, come sit down, and tell me what happened."

Connie joins Janice on a bench nearby. "I'm sorry I took him over there, but he said it would only be for a short moment and that he needed to pick up some things."

"My dear girl, you have nothing to be sorry for, but his dad will be sorry when I get my hands on him."

"Please, ma'am, don't do anything that you may regret."

"Trust me—what I'm going to do to him, I will never regret.

He has put his hands on me for a long time, and I did nothing because I loved him, and he always apologized, but this time, no apologies will be accepted. That is my child in there, and I will protect him even if it kills me."

Just as Connie begins to tell the whole story of what led up to her and AJ's mom sitting outside the hospital, AJ's dad pulls up. He gets out of the car, taking unstable steps that let Connie and Janice know he is still drunk. He dons a look of concern when he spots the two women sitting near the emergency entrance. As he approaches, Janice clutches her purse tightly and looks over to Connie.

Janice whispers to Connie, "Baby, I think you should go and see Anthony Jr. now. He's in room 307."

Connie musters up her courage. "I'm sorry, ma'am, but I don't want to leave you here alone with him."

"It's okay, Connie. I'll take care of this."

Connie glances toward AJ's dad, who is slowly lumbering their way. "Ma'am, what are you planning to do?"

"Don't worry. Just tell Anthony Jr. I'll be in shortly."

"Yes ma'am," Connie relents. She steps through the hospital doors. Then she turns and looks back at AJ's mom and dad with a sense of wonder filling her.

As the emergency doors close and shut off her view of them, a sense of fright washes over her. Connie's first thought is to go back outside and stand with AJ's mom because she has seen the anger that is present in Anthony Sr., but then she thinks, "We are at the hospital. He's not crazy enough to try anything here with all the police around." With that in mind, she heads to the elevator to go find AJ's room.

When she finds room 307, she raps her knuckles against the door.

"AJ, I hope you are decent, 'cause I'm coming in!" she calls.

"Girl, come on in here! Somehow I knew you would be here soon."

Connie steps into the room and approaches AJ's bedside. "No, you didn't. You don't know me like that."

"Actually, I do."

"Oh, really? You think you do!" Connie then lightly thumps AJ on his head and says, "Did you know I was going to do that? Bet you didn't."

"Con, what you do that for?" AJ puts his hand to his head. "You do know I'm here 'cause I have a concussion?"

"Boy, your mom said you are all right, so stop milking it, and get your butt out that bed," Connie states as she walks to the window. She can see AJ's parents down below, near the entrance where she came in.

"Did you come to see me or just stare out the window? What's so important out there anyway?" AJ asks.

"Oh, nothing. Just wanted to look out the window. Is that a problem? 'Cause if it is, I'll just push you out of it," Connie says as she starts to laugh.

"There you go, being violent again." AJ shakes his head.

Connie closes the curtains. "There—are you happy now?"

"Very," AJ says sarcastically.

"Are you gonna get out that bed so I can take you home, or do I need to tell the doctor you need a shot in your butt?"

"Dang girl, why you so pushy?"

"I'm not. I just don't like hospitals," Connie says as she glances toward the covered window.

AJ frowns. "What is so important out there that you can't stop looking at it?"

"I'll tell you if you promise not to get mad at me."

"Why would I get mad at you?"

"'Cause I did something I promised I wouldn't do."

"Con . . . what did you do?"

"Promise you won't get mad?"

"Girl, I promise. Now what did you do?"

"Well, I keep looking out the window 'cause your mom is out there with your dad."

"Why would I be mad at you about that?"

Connie bites her lip and hesitates, then says, "'Cause I told your mom what happened this morning and how you ended up here."

"Con, why would you do that?" AJ drops his head back against the headboard.

"Your mom called him to take y'all home, so I had to tell her."

AJ gets up and walks to the window. He pulls aside the curtain and peers out to see his mom and dad arguing. He quickly turns to Connie and says, "I have to get down there. He's still drunk, and you've seen he doesn't care about anyone but himself."

Connie grabs his arm before he can leave. "AJ, what are you gonna do besides end up back in here if he decides to swing on you again?"

"I promise not to let things get that far. We just got to get my mom away from him." AJ looks back out the window and sees his mom reaching into her purse as his dad, with fists clenched, stands in a posture that indicates he's ready to strike.

AJ swiftly turns and darts out the room, with Connie right behind him.

"AJ, wait!" she screams, but her screams are ignored as AJ makes his way to the elevator and quickly gets in. Connie manages to join him in the elevator before the doors can close.

AJ and Connie finally make it down to the lobby. Just in time, too, because as they reach the exit, they can see AJ's dad raise his hand to strike AJ's mom, but she steps back and pulls a gun from her purse. AJ begins running toward his mom, screaming her name, as Connie turns and runs back inside to get help from hospital security.

AJ makes it to his mom and dad just as Connie makes it to the security desk and explains what is going on outside of the emergency entrance. The security guard calls the police before heading out to stop anything else from happening.

AJ jumps in between his parents and pleads with his mom to put the gun away. His dad, still drunk, says, "Move out the way, and let that bitch shoot me. That lil' shit ain't gonna do nothing but piss me off even more."

"Dad, shut up and just leave, okay?" Keeping his dad in his peripheral vision, AJ turns his focus to his mom. "Mom, please put the gun down. I'm sure the police have already been called, and you know they are not going to care that you are trying to protect me, and all they are going to see is another black person with a gun. Mom, please. Too many black people have died by police lately. I don't want you nor I to be next, so please ignore Dad just for the moment, and put the gun down."

His dad scoffs. "You can't ignore me. You *need* me 'cause y'all are nothing without me."

AJ glances back at his dad. "No, Dad, you are wrong. We are nothing but punching bags with you, but we will be so much more without you, so why don't you just get out of here and leave us alone?"

His mom reluctantly places the gun back in her purse and hands the purse over to AJ just as the security guard comes running with his gun drawn, yelling, "Where is the gun? Get on the ground! Get on the ground! Where is the gun?" He points his gun at AJ and his mother.

AJ throws his hands up. "Sir, please don't shoot! The gun is in my mom's purse! I can toss it over to you if you want!"

"Drop the purse, and kick it over to me, and get on the ground!"

AJ's dad starts laughing. "Look at you two. Y'all better do what he says and get dirty."

The security guard turns toward AJ's dad and points his gun at him. "Sir, you need to get on the ground too!"

"I'll be damned if I get on the ground. You better shoot me 'cause that's the only way I'm getting down there."

"Sir, please don't shoot him," AJ pleads as he drops to his knees. "He's drunk." He turns to his dad. "Dad, do what he says. Just get on the ground."

The police finally arrive and make their way through a crowd of spectators and place handcuffs on both of AJ's parents as AJ watches helplessly, still on his knees.

AJ speaks up, "Why are you arresting her? She was only protecting herself from him! Dad, tell them what happened!"

"She was going to shoot me, so let them take her to jail."

An onlooker nearby yells out, "The young man is telling the truth! I started recording with my phone after he pushed her."

An officer steps toward the onlooker. "Sir, I am going to need to see that video."

"Sure. It's right here, clear as day."

"You have video showing my mom was protecting herself, so can you please let her go?" AJ's voice cracks in his desperate plea.

"I'm sorry, son, but it's still against the law to have a gun on government property."

AJ's mom speaks up, her voice weary. "I have a license for the gun, but it's at home. I only got it to protect us from him. I don't even like guns." AJ can hardly believe what he's hearing—his mom has been keeping this even from him?

"Sorry, but you have to go," the officer responds to AJ's mom. "Based on everything we have, I'm sure the DA won't prosecute you, and you should be released in a few hours, but he"—the officer gestures to Anthony Sr.—"on the other hand, will be charged with simple assault and domestic battery for pushing and attempting to hit you."

"Will the charges stick this time?" AJ asks, not ready to get his hopes up that things might change.

"With this video, I'm sure they will. Now, son, do you have someone that can take you home?"

AJ nods. "Yes, my friend is here. She can take me home, then take me to pick up my mom."

"Where is your friend now?"

AJ points to Connie a few yards away. "That's her over there, talking to the other officer."

"Okay, you two go home and get your mother's permit, and by the time you make it to the station, your mom should be ready to go." The officer pauses and then adds, "Oh, but first you might want to go back in and change." He gestures to AJ's hospital gown.

AJ nods and then jogs over to Connie. "Con, I'll be back. I need to go change into my clothes."

"So now you want to go change? I tried to tell you your bony little butt was showing before you came out here. And it's such a cute butt."

"*Really*, Con? You got jokes now?"

"Well, it is." She shrugs nonchalantly.

"Will you stop looking at my butt and go get the car?" He tries to turn and walk away before she can say anything else.

"Hey, AJ, guess what?"

He sighs and turns back to her. "What now?"

"That guy has your butt on video!" Connie says with a giggle.

"Ha ha. Not funny," AJ replies before turning away for good this time.

***

AJ and Connie leave the hospital, heading back to Darlene's house to find his mom's gun permit. Along the way, Connie looks over at AJ and says, "That was very intense. I thought she was gonna shoot him for real."

Looking out the window, AJ states, "She probably would have if I hadn't made it down there in time."

"At least with that video, your dad won't be bothering you guys for a while."

"Yeah, and we can finally be at peace without the worry of his attacks on us, and I can go off to college knowing my mom is safe."

"Speaking of college," Connie says, "you are this year's salutatorian. Through all that has been going on, have you had a chance to work on your speech for graduation?"

AJ shrugs. "I started on it but haven't had a chance to finish it."

"How much have you written so far?"

"Not much at all. I don't know what to say."

"*You*, of all people, don't know what to say?" Connie asks with a smirk.

AJ glances her way with narrowed eyes. "What is that supposed to mean?"

"Just that if something needs to be said, you have been very outspoken through the years at school. Now that you have the chance to speak on behalf of the James Madison High graduates of 2016, you have nothing to say."

AJ exhales loudly. "Okay, I get it. Well, as soon as we get my mom and make sure she is all right, I'll calm down and get my thoughts together and figure out what I want to say."

Connie and AJ finally make it to Darlene's house, and as they approach the front door, Darlene meets them and says, "Your mom just called and wanted me to give you these papers. She is waiting on you to bring them to her at the police station. What is going on now? Did your dad do something to her?" Darlene's eyes dart between the two kids as she waits for an answer.

Connie responds, "There was an altercation at the hospital. She was about to shoot him, and they both got taken to the station."

Darlene places a hand over her chest. "Oh my. Is Janice okay?"

Connie nods. "Yes ma'am. She is. We just need to take these papers down there to show the gun is registered to her and that she has a license to carry."

"How about I take the papers and pick her up, and you two go inside and eat?" Darlene offers. "I just finished cooking smothered pork chops, hot-water corn bread, mashed potatoes, candied yams, corn on the cob, and purple hull peas."

AJ says, "Dang, Aunt Darlene. Are you expecting the army to come by and eat all that food you cooked?"

"No, but everybody knows if you are hungry, Aunt Darlene will feed you. Now y'all get on in there and fix y'all a plate. And, Anthony, don't eat all the banana pudding. I'll be back with your mama in a little while."

AJ and Connie head into the house. Then Connie stops and looks strangely at AJ as he keeps walking.

He turns back to her. "Con, what are you waiting for? Girl, come on here."

Connie starts laughing but tries to hide it.

"What's so funny now?" AJ asks and then sighs.

"Oh, nothing," she replies.

"Yeah, I bet nothing."

"If you must know, I was laughing at you."

AJ peers at her suspiciously. "What *about* me?"

"If only you could have seen what I saw when you was running with that gown just blowing in the wind."

With a roll of the eyes, AJ replies, "Ha ha, still not funny."

Connie continues to chuckle. "Oh, yes it is, bony butt."

"Keep on, and—"

"And *what*?"

"Nothing," AJ mutters.

"Yeah, that's what I thought."

AJ turns and walks toward the kitchen. "Will you just come on in here and fix you a plate, girl?"

Connie takes a whiff of the air. "That food does smell good. Okay, I'll leave you alone for now, Mr. Bony Butt."

"See, there you go again."

"Well, I can't help it. You know how I am."

"Can we eat without any more butt jokes? *Please?*"

Connie waves a hand at him. "All right, boy. Don't be getting all in your feelings."

CHAPTER FOUR

NORTHWEST SUBSTATION OF THE
DALLAS POLICE DEPARTMENT
LATER THAT DAY

Darlene arrives at the police station with the gun permit in hand. She walks up to the officer at the front desk and says, "Here is the gun permit for Mrs. Janice Harris. Now can she go home?"

The officer takes the papers from her and briefly reads over the name on the permit. "I'm sorry, ma'am—there must be some misunderstanding. Mrs. Harris is not under arrest. She is free to leave. We just needed to see her gun permit, but the DA has declined to charge her with any wrongdoing on her part."

"Well, where is she?"

"She is speaking with the DA about the incident at the hospital. Her husband, on the other hand, is not free to go."

Darlene scoffs. "Who cares about that asshole? Y'all should just leave his ass in a cell with a big ole dude that hates women beaters. That would be a great deal of justice. Now can you let my friend know I am here to take her home?"

Not long after, Janice walks out to the lobby, still a little shaken up over the day's events. She hugs Darlene tightly.

Darlene holds her friend close. "Girl, are you all right? What happened at that hospital that you had to pull your gun?"

Janice shakes her head. "Can we talk about it later? I just want to get out of here and go home."

"Sure, baby. Let's get out of here." She leads Janice to her car. On the drive home, they ride in silence for a while until Darlene says, "Whatever he did that made you pull out your gun, you should've shot him. Hell, he was already at the hospital—he wouldn't have far to go for treatment."

Janice cracks a smile. "If Anthony Jr. hadn't stepped in, I would have. I would have shot him right between the eyes. Hell, girl, he wouldn't need a hospital then—he'd need a coroner."

"See, there you go—that's the beautiful smile I like to see on your face," Darlene replies. "We better hurry up and get to the house if you want some of that good cooking I made. Your son and his friend are there, and you know that boy can eat—just like my Kevin."

"Darlene, you know the first thing I want to do when we get to the house?"

"What's that?"

"Relax in a hot bath and read one of my son's poems."

Darlene nods approvingly. "Girl, I'm sure he has one that would help put your mind at ease."

When Janice and Darlene pull into the driveway, AJ bolts out the door and hugs his mom the moment she gets out of the car. He hugs her like he has never before.

Janice says, "Baby, I'm okay, but can you loosen up? 'Cause now *you* are choking *me*."

AJ pulls back. "Sorry, Mom, but I was so worried about you."

"It's okay, son. We are going to be okay now."

"Mom, let's go in, and I'll fix you a plate." He turns toward the front door to lead the way.

Janice starts to follow him, but she says, "I'd like that, son, but first I'd love to read one of your poems while I relax in a nice hot bath."

AJ smiles meekly at her. "I believe I have one you would love. I'll get it while your water is running for your bath." Once inside the house, AJ digs through his backpack, searching for that one certain poem he has in mind, but he can't find it.

Connie wanders over to him. "Which poem are you looking for? 'Cause I still have a few in my car that you left the other night."

"There are actually two that I'm looking for. One is called 'Truthfulness of Pain.' The other is 'An Angel Walks Amongst Us.'"

Connie nods. "Yeah, both of those are in my car. I'll go get them."

"Thanks, Con."

***

As AJ's mom settles into her bath, Darlene brings the poems to her and lights an aroma candle to help her relax even more. Janice places a rolled-up towel behind her neck and leans back so that she is almost submerged in the tub. She thanks Darlene for all she is doing for her and AJ. Then she closes her eyes and slowly drifts away to a place where she can hear the rushing waters of a waterfall, birds chirping, and the rustle of the leaves as a cool breeze comes through. After a good thirty minutes of just silence and clearing her mind, she sits up and grabs AJ's poems. The title "Truthfulness of Pain" catches her eye, so she decides to read that one first.

Truthfulness of Pain

My pain runs deep.

It touches my soul.

It hides from seeing eyes.

My pain lurks in the darkness.

It peeks its head out when I'm alone.

It speaks to me in a whisper.

My pain fills my sky with gloom.

It blocks the sun from shining through.

It showers my days with rain.

The truthfulness of my pain is that

It's killing me.

It's draining my will.

The truthfulness of my pain is that

Despair is among us all.

It's filling our lives.

It's overtaking our happiness.

The truthfulness of my pain

    Is living a life

        Without you, Mom . . .

Janice wipes tears from her eyes and takes a deep breath before reading the next poem. She thinks to herself, "How could I have let a man keep me from recognizing how much pain my son was in? How could I have been so blind to the fact that my son is a talented writer? That stops here and now."

Still wiping tears from her eyes, Janice begins to read the second poem.

An Angel Walks Amongst Us

There are footsteps beside you

    Although you can't see them.

You are embraced by loving arms

    Although you can't feel them.

Your spirit is carried over rough terrain

    Although you are on solid ground.

An angel walks with us.

Your burdens shall be lifted

    Although your heart still feels pain.

Your troubles will be washed away

    With the next day's rain

And you shall shine

Like the sun's rays.

Your life is covered with God's blood

Although you venture through

Life's hardships.

An angel walks amongst us

To secure our days

And guide us through the night.

Although your angel is not seen

He is still walking with you . . .

As Janice clutches the poem tightly, Darlene knocks on the door and calls out, "Baby girl, are you okay in there?"

Trying not to sound like she's been crying, Janice replies, "Yes, I'm okay! I'll be out shortly."

"Take as much time as you need. I'll put your plate to the side, and I'll make sure Anthony saves you some banana pudding. You know that's his favorite."

Janice cracks a little smile. "Thank you, sis."

"You're welcome, girl. I'll let you get back to relaxing, okay, Jan?"

Janice leans back in the tub again, closes her eyes, and thinks of all the times she missed out on something special in her son's life because of the shame she had for herself and because trying to cover the bruises had become a daunting task. Sitting there in the tub, she promises herself that for the most important day of her son's life this far, she will be there—to see him walk across that stage to graduate and to give a speech to his graduating class.

Janice gathers her emotions and readies herself to step out of the bath a new woman. No more neglecting her son's talents. No more being ashamed. No more feeling unworthy. And definitely no more abuse.

She is ready to take back control of her life.

When Janice leaves the bathroom and rejoins Darlene, Darlene looks her over with wide eyes.

Darlene says, "Girl, what did you do in there? Or better yet, where did your mind take you? 'Cause whatever you did, or wherever your mind took you, I wanna know."

"Darlene, what are you talking about?"

"You are glowing! You seem to be a different person than when you went in."

Janice smiles ever so softly. "I just sat back and finally relaxed my mind, and my son's poetry helped with that. I realized that if I have to be hit by a man to learn that he loves me, then hell, I'll just love on myself."

"Do I need to hide my batteries?"

"Girl, be quiet! I'm not talking like that."

"Well, hell, you might want to try it. It works for me."

"Darlene, stop being nasty. I'm going to go eat and leave your nasty mind in here by yourself."

"That's fine . . . I'll be in here relaxing with Bob."

"Girl, who is Bob?" Janice asks skeptically.

"Oh, he's my battery-operated boyfriend."

"Darlene, you just nasty." Janice shakes her head.

"Yep! Nasty as I wanna be, you mean. Ms. Millie Jackson learned from me, baby."

"Bye, girl. I'm going to go eat and have a glass of wine."

As Janice enters the kitchen, she overhears Connie and AJ talking.

She announces her presence by saying, "Excuse me, guys. What are we talking about in here?"

"Nothing really, Mom," AJ states as he gets up and offers his seat to his mother.

Connie clarifies, "Ma'am, we are talking about graduation and AJ's speech. He said as soon as he knows you are all right that he will start working on it. But now he acts like he can't think of anything to say."

Janice looks at her son. "Anthony, baby, I'm okay. All you need to worry about is your speech. You know what to say. Just listen to your heart, and it will all come together just like your poetry, which I love, by the way."

AJ kisses his mom on her forehead and tells Connie, "You said you would help me write this speech, so now I'm taking you up on it. Let's go figure this out."

"Boy, who are you ordering around like that? Boy, don't let your mom see you get tore up!"

Janice laughs softly. "Oh, Anthony, I like her. You better change your tone with her, though. She is feisty."

AJ and Connie head off to the living room to work on his speech.

"Okay, Mr. Bony Butt, what do you have written so far?"

"I'm not showing you if you're gonna start that *bony butt* stuff again."

"Fine. I'll just go home. I need my beauty sleep anyway." Connie stands dramatically.

"All right, fine. Here you go. It's only a few lines anyway."

Connie plops back down on the couch and reads what AJ has written. Then she tears the paper up.

"Con, what did you do that for?"

"'Cause you can do better. That was something my nephew would write if he had to write a graduation speech, and he's in the fourth grade."

"Well, why don't you write it if you think you can do better?"

"*Think?* Boy, please. I *know* I can do better than that, but I'm not the one giving a speech. So shut up, and start writing."

"Dang, why you gotta be so mean?"

"'Cause I am. Wanna make something of it?"

"You know what, Con—"

"What, boy?"

"One of these days, I'mma—"

"You gonna what?"

"I'm gonna go ahead and write this speech." AJ gathers up the torn bits of paper.

"Yeah, I thought that's what you was gonna say."

AJ whispers under his breath, "You know you not the boss of me."

"I heard that!" Connie huffs. "And yes, I am. Now shut up, and start writing. We have a few weeks left before graduation, so this speech better be ready, and it better be good, or you gonna be in some real trouble with me."

"Again, when did we get married? 'Cause you talk to me like you my wife and like I'm your wimpy husband."

"No, you just a wimp."

"I feel for your husband when you do get married," AJ says as he busts out laughing.

"Oh, that's funny to you! You had a small concussion—don't make me give you a big one."

AJ's mom ducks her head into the living room. "Do you guys need anything to drink before I head off to bed?"

Connie perks up. "No ma'am. We are okay."

"All right. Don't stay up too late. Connie, if you are staying over, Anthony knows where the extra blankets are."

"If it's okay with you and my mom, I wouldn't mind staying to help AJ with his speech."

Janice nods. "Okay, give her a call, and if it's okay with her, I'm fine with it. Besides, Connie, if you weren't here helping, Anthony would probably wait till graduation day to finish."

"Good night, *Mom*," AJ says with kind of a stern voice.

"I'm going! Don't be all in your feelings, boy."

"Ha ha, that's what I said to him earlier," Connie replies, looking pleased with herself.

"Can we focus on the speech now, Con?" AJ pleads.

"Boy, hush. Don't you see grown folks talking?"

"Wait . . . I'm older than you."

"Only in age, baby, only in age."

"So, Con, what are you trying to say?"

She shrugs. "Just that I'm more mature and wiser than you."

"Oh, really?"

"Yes, really, AJ!"

Janice giggles over the conversation and states, "I'll let you kids get back to writing that speech. Good night, Anthony. And good night to you, Ms. Connie. Don't forget to call your mom."

Connie nods eagerly. "Yes ma'am. I'm about to call her now." As Janice heads upstairs, Connie turns to AJ. "AJ, I'm going to step out and call my mom. You get to work writing, and you already know if I don't like it, you will start over."

"Yes, Teach, I know."

"Don't be a smart-ass, or I'll have to kick your ass."

"Con, you know I'm not gonna let you keep talking smack to me."

"Boy, boo—you can talk that shit all you want. You ain't gonna do shit."

AJ picks up a pillow and tosses it at Connie. "Girl, just go make your call so we can get back to work."

"If you planned to hit me with that pillow, you might want to put on your glasses, 'cause I'm way over here, and you threw that pillow toward the TV."

"Oh, hush. If I wanted to hit you with it, I would have."

"Yeah, right. Boy, you are blind as a bat."

***

While Connie is on the phone with her mom, AJ receives a call from his dad. As soon as he hears his dad's voice, he instinctively wants to hang up but instead decides to hear what he has to say.

Reluctantly, AJ asks, "What is it that you want?"

"I've sobered up and just wanted to say I'm sorry."

"You know what, man?" AJ tries to keep his voice steady. "I'm not trying to hear that, 'cause I've heard it all before. You said that after breaking Mom's jaw. You said it after breaking down the front door. You said it after kicking Mom in the ribs. But you know what you have never said? You have never said that you was gonna quit drinking. You never said you have a problem with anger. You never said that you needed help. So all that 'I'm sorry' mess is just a tactic to get sympathy, but you get none of that here."

"You're right, son." His dad's voice is quiet and meek.

"Naw, man. Don't do that—don't call me *son*." AJ shakes his head vigorously, pacing back and forth as he grips the phone. "You lost that privilege a long time ago."

"But I—"

"But you *nothing*, man, and that's what you are to me. *Nothing!*"

His dad clears his throat before speaking again. "I'll be in here for some time, and—"

"And that's good," AJ snaps. "That's where you belong. Get some help while you are in there. Do some type of AA and anger management. Man, don't you know any one of those blows my mom took from you could have ended her life?"

"Yes, I do, and if I could take it all back, I would."

"That's what every guy in jail says because they are locked behind those bars, and all that is just jailhouse talk 'cause if you meant that, there wouldn't have been a tenth time of me picking my mom up off the floor and wiping the blood-filled tears from her face. Hell, man, if you really loved her, there wouldn't have even been a first time. Until you get some type of help, don't call me anymore."

"Could you please tell your mom I called?"

"*Hell* no!" AJ exclaims right before hanging up.

Connie walks back in the room and asks AJ who he was just going off on.

AJ replies, "Take a wild guess."

"Who? Your father?"

"He ain't no father," AJ vents, still pacing. "A father respects his wife and kids."

"Well, was it your dad?"

"He ain't that either. A dad teaches his kid how to be a man, not a woman beater. Like I said before, he is just a sperm donor."

"What did he want this time?"

"He wanted to give a fake apology, but I told him I didn't want to hear that shit."

"Yeah, I heard you all the way down the hall. I'm surprised your mom didn't come back down."

"I'm glad she didn't. I don't want to see her upset or crying again. I wouldn't be able to handle that."

"She seemed so happy tonight," Connie responds gently.

"Yeah, she did, and I miss seeing her smile. Tonight I saw a glimmer of that woman I remember from when I was a little kid."

"AJ, I think your poems helped put that smile on your mom's lips tonight."

AJ stops pacing and abruptly sits on the couch. "Okay, Con, enough of this mushy stuff. Let's get back to the speech. I think I know what I want to say to our peers and parents."

"It better be better than that stuff you wrote at first." Connie joins him on the couch. "So let me hear what you have so far."

"Can you wait till I'm finished?"

"Nope! I have to make sure it's good enough. Since you called me *Teach*, that's exactly what I'm gonna act like, so start reading, young man."

As AJ begins to read out loud, Connie stops him and instructs him to stand up and read his speech as if it were graduation day. "Put some feeling into it, and project it so that people way up in the stands can hear you, and don't stand there like you have stage fright."

"Con, you do realize I have been in theater class since fourth grade?"

"What does that have to do with this?"

"I'm just saying I am used to being on stage, so I know how to get my message across."

"This is way different than that. You are not doing a performance—you will have to get everyone's attention only on you and what you have to say for about fifteen minutes, but it's gonna seem like forever."

"Don't worry. I got this."

"You better have it! I'm not gonna be able to come and rescue you this time."

AJ narrows his eyes. "When did you ever have to come and rescue me?"

"Oh, how can you forget when you had to do a solo for the MLK parade, and you forgot the song, so I had to jump in and start playing."

"Naw, I don't remember nothing like that."

"Damn, that concussion must have given you memory loss. Maybe we need to take you back to the hospital."

"There you go, trying to be funny again."

"Trying? I *am* funny. Kevin Hart gets some of his best stuff from me."

"Yeah, right. You wish. Maybe you're the one that needs to go get checked out, 'cause you are delusional."

"Boy, shut up and read."

"Now how am I gonna do that? Do you want me to shut up or read?"

"Do both—shut up talking smack before I smack you, and read the damn speech."

"Okay, Ms. Bossy. You don't have to be so rude. You know, Con, I told you one of these days, I'm gonna win one of these little spats we have."

"And I told you that you will win when I let you, and guess what? Today is not that day."

"All right, Ms. Smarty-Pants."

"Better to be known as smarty-pants than bony butt."

"See, why do you always have to have the last word?"

"'Cause I do and always will."

AJ's mom peeks her head around the corner. "Anthony, what are you guys still doing up?"

"Sorry, Mom. Did we wake you up?"

"No, baby. I was just getting up to get me something to drink."

"We are just finishing up with the speech," AJ answers.

Janice turns to Connie. "Connie, did you call your mom?"

"Yes ma'am. She said it was okay to stay over this time."

"All right. You guys better get some rest. Anthony, baby, how are you feeling?"

"I'm feeling fine, and Mom, can you not call me baby?"

"Well, you are my baby boy . . . no matter how old you get."

Connie smiles. "Yeah, AJ, let her have that. I think it's cute."

Janice starts back toward the stairs. "Okay, you guys, I'm going back to bed, and y'all should too. Anthony, show Connie where everything is and where she can sleep, and if you are not feeling up to going to school in the morning, it will be okay if you stay at home."

"Mom, I'm feeling fine," AJ insists. "Stop worrying. Besides, I still have to turn in some papers for college applications." His mom accepts his answer and heads off to bed.

Connie faces AJ. "Hey, AJ, you know Ms. Allie is going to want to talk to you about what happened today when you go to turn those papers in tomorrow, and that would be as good a time as any to talk to her about it."

"Yeah, I know, but everything is over now since he is in jail."

"No buts, AJ. Promise me you will talk to her if she asks. Just because he is in jail now doesn't mean everything you and your mom have been through is over. Stuff like this doesn't go away overnight."

"And Con, how would you know? You live in a happy home."

"It's happy now, but my mom used to tell me stories of how when she was growing up, her best friend killed herself to escape the abuse she received from her dad, and guess what? Although it wasn't my mom who was abused, she still to this day feels the pain from losing her best friend because of domestic violence. She still wakes up in a cold sweat because she has nightmares about what she could have done to help. No one was there for them to talk to, but you have someone that can help you or at least talk you through what you're feeling when you think you can't deal."

"Con, that's what you are here for."

"True, but I don't know how to give you the advice you need or point you in a direction for help except to her."

"I'm getting sleepy, so can we talk about this in the morning on the way to school?"

"Oh, so you want to shut down on me when the conversation gets serious? I'm not letting you go to sleep till you promise to talk to her if she asks."

"Okay, I promise. Now can we get some sleep?"

CHAPTER FIVE

DARLENE'S HOME

THE NEXT DAY

The next morning, Janice goes to wake AJ and Connie for school, but they have already gotten up and are ready to get the day started.

Connie pokes AJ. "Remember, AJ, you made a promise to talk to Ms. Allie."

AJ bats away Connie's poking finger. "Yeah, I remember, but only if she asks. I'm definitely not going to just offer up information to her, though."

"I'll go with you if you want me to."

"Naw, I'm good. Besides, I might not even see her."

"How are you planning to do that? You have to turn those papers in to her."

"I might just email a copy to her."

"You mean to tell me you could have emailed it to her? Then why did we need to go get them from the house yesterday?"

"I didn't have a copy saved to my computer then, but I saved one last night just in case."

"Oh, so you was trying to be slick and find a way to renege on your promise?"

"No, I just was trying to find a way to get them to her in case I didn't go to school today."

Connie studies his sincere expression for a moment, then says, "Well, AJ, you are going, so there is no excuse not to see her, and if she wants to talk about your situation, please don't say everything is okay, 'cause you know it's not."

"Yes ma'am," AJ replies with a smug look.

"I saw that look, and don't make me read you this early in the morning, boy."

"There you go, already starting."

"Ain't nobody starting nothing. You just best not give me that look again, or I will start something."

"Con, you are a mess."

"No, I am not, but I will mess that eye up if you keep talking smack."

AJ turns and walks out of the room and mumbles under his breath, "Dang, why you always wanna hit somebody?"

"I heard that!" Connie calls out, following him from the room. "And I don't always wanna hit somebody—just you when you get out of line."

AJ yells back over his shoulder on his way to the kitchen, "Ain't nobody in front of me or behind me, so where is the line?"

"Boy, don't get smart with me."

"Hey, Con, we in the same classes, so I can't help but to get smart with you unless you want me to not pay attention in class."

Connie follows him into the kitchen and hurls a pillow at AJ, catching him right in the back of the head. "Now that's how you throw a pillow at someone!" she states, trying to hold in her laughter. "Bet you stop trying to be a smart-ass now, won't you?"

Darlene walks into the kitchen. "What are you guys doing, and why haven't y'all left for school?" She starts making coffee for her and Janice.

AJ replies, "We are getting ready to go as soon as Con stops throwing things at me."

"I'll stop throwing stuff at you when you stop getting smart with me."

"Can we just go before we are late, Ms. Connie Smalls?"

"Boy, boo! Don't call my name out like that."

"Why? Are you wanted by police?"

"Not yet, but keep on, and I will be."

"So what you saying? You gonna kill me?"

"Naw, but probably just maim you a little, like cut off a toe or two. You know—something that can't be noticed easy."

AJ turns to Darlene. "You hear that, Aunt Darlene? She talking about cutting off my toe."

"Well, at least it's not way north of your toe and south of your stomach—now that would be more than maiming you," Darlene retorts.

"That's not funny, Aunt Darlene!"

"Hey, I'm just saying."

Connie leans against the kitchen counter. "Yeah, AJ, it's not like you need that anyway."

"Wow, really? I can't win around you women. Can we go to school now? *Please?*"

"There you go, getting in your feelings again." Connie rolls her eyes. "Dang, we just playing with you."

"You don't play about cutting off a man's wang. That's the no-play zone."

"All right, crybaby, let's go."

AJ heaves a sigh of relief. "Thank you, Con. See you later, Aunt Darlene, and tell Mom I'll see her when school's out."

Darlene smiles his way. "Okay, baby, I will, and you call us if you start to not feel well."

"I will, but I promise I feel fine."

Darlene immediately turns to Connie. "Connie, he's a bit stubborn, so will you call us if you see him acting strange?"

"Yes ma'am, but I think he's always acting strange."

"Well, stranger than usual, then."

"Okay, I will."

AJ shuffles back and forth uneasily. "Con, it's getting late. School starts in thirty minutes."

"Boy, since when are you in such a rush to get to school?"

"Since my aunty and my mom got on your side."

"You just mad 'cause like Michael Jackson said in *The Wiz*, 'You can't win.'"

"Ha ha, you still not funny," AJ replies.

* * *

With the kids finally off to school, Darlene and Janice sit down to breakfast to talk about yesterday's events.

"Janice, girl, I wish I could have been there when you pulled that gun out of your purse. I'm sure he damned near pissed his pants. What made you take the gun with you yesterday?"

"After thinking about how his anger gets the best of him, and I get the worst, I knew I had to protect myself from his next attack. I promised myself that he would never get the chance to smack me around again."

"Well, lucky for you that you went the right way of getting the gun and permit, 'cause if you had mine, your butt would be gone."

"Darlene, are you telling me your gun is illegal?"

"Oh no, my gun is legal, but them bullets not."

Janice tilts her head questioningly. "What you mean the bullets are not legal?"

"Let's just say you can get five years per bullet if you are caught with them."

Janice's jaw drops a little. "Darlene, where on earth did you get your hands on something like that? And why?"

"Girl, I know people. Besides, we in the hood. If someone comes after me, I wanna make sure I can stop any advances. Anyway, enough about me—what are you going to do now that he is finally locked up?"

Janice leans back and lets out a pent-up breath. "Live a wonderful and stress-free life. But first I'm going to eat whatever it is that you cooked, 'cause it smells so good, girl. My stomach been over here just growling the whole time we been talking."

Darlene waves away the compliment. "Oh, it's just a lil' something I put together."

"You sure made a lot. Who else is coming to eat with us?"

"No one. I make a lot every morning to take to the guys down by the park. They don't have much, so I help out the best I can, and they say breakfast is the most important meal of the day."

"With all this food, you can feed the whole neighborhood. What is it all, anyway?"

"Just some cheese grits, scrambled eggs with onions and bell peppers, grilled smoked sausage, pancakes with different fruit toppings, and some breakfast chops."

"Why cook so many different things?"

"You gotta give the people choices. If not, and they only have one choice, it might be good for some but not for others."

Janice peers at her friend. "Why do I feel everything you do has a life lesson in it somewhere?"

Darlene laughs at the question before responding, "'Cause it usually does. But why do I feel like you smoothly changed the subject off of you and onto my food?"

"Did I really?"

"Yes, you did!"

"Girl, I didn't even notice." Janice laughs.

"Yeah, right, you didn't notice. By the way, Anthony Jr. said he will see you after school, and Connie said thank you for letting her stay over so they could work on some speech. Anthony has his hands full with that one. How long have they been dating?"

"They're not dating."

"Could have fooled me."

"No, seriously—they are just really close friends."

"Yeah, right, and Bob is just a back massager."

Janice shakes her head insistently. "No. Darlene, we are not going to bring up Bob, not while I'm eating."

"Ooh, *girrrl*, Bob had me feeling real good last night."

Janice shoves her plate away. "Okay, I'm done eating. I don't want to hear about your sexual deeds with Bob."

"Janice, I'm telling you—get you one. He'll make you purr like a kitten."

"Shouldn't you be going to work with your nasty self?"

"Nope, I'm off, but I should be getting down to the park and setting up before it gets crowded. Wanna come with?"

"Only if we don't have to talk about your nasty battery-operated boyfriend."

"We don't have to, but if you see me twitch, don't worry—I'm just still feeling the aftershock."

"You just nasty, Darlene, just plain ole nasty, nasty, nasty."

***

Connie and AJ make it to school with ten minutes left before the first bell rings.

"Now, boy, I told you we wouldn't be late."

"We almost was!" AJ huffs.

"Almost don't count, though."

"Will you just park so we can get to class?"

"You know, you can just roll your ass right on out the door if you are in that big of a hurry. I said we will get here on time—I didn't say we would be in class on time."

"Really, Con?"

"Boy, I'm about to park, so stop whining like a lil' bi-atch."

"I'm just ready to get this day over with. That's all."

"Whateva'. Just remember to take those papers to Ms. Allie and talk to her about what's going on with you and your mom."

"Yeah, okay," AJ responds.

"Don't play with me, boy. You better open your mouth and talk if she ask you anything about yesterday."

"Yes ma'am."

"Don't *ma'am* me!"

"Stop acting like my mom, then."

"Just get out the damn car, and go see her."

"Yes—"

"If you say *ma'am*, I'mma bust you upside your head to the white meat."

"Damn, when did Bernie Mac get in the car?"

"Your smart ass got ten seconds to start running to that front before I get out this car and kick your ass."

AJ swings the door open and hops out. "See, Con, you sound just like my mom."

"Boy, just go. I'm coming right behind you soon as I finish my makeup, and you better go straight to Ms. Allie's office."

AJ says under his breath, "Yes ma'am."

"Boy, don't think I didn't hear that, 'cause I did."

AJ heads on into school, and just as he makes it to the door, it swings open, and there stands Ms. Allie.

She smiles at him. "I saw you from my office and wanted to be sure I caught you before class."

"Ms. Allie, I was just heading to your office to turn in these college papers."

"Thanks, Anthony. I've been waiting on those, but I would really like to talk to you about yesterday."

AJ stares at the ground. "I know. I had a feeling that you would."

"The school officer would like to sit in on our conversation as well, if you don't mind."

"Do I really have a choice?"

"Yes, Anthony, you do, but we would like to know what is going on so that we could help or get you the help you need. Can we step into my office and finish this discussion?"

"We can, Ms. Allie, but the problem is really already taken care of," he insists.

"Let's talk more about it when we get in my office. The school officer is already in there, but I can ask him to leave if you feel more comfortable with just you and I talking."

AJ thinks about his promise to Connie to at least give it a shot. "It's okay, Ms. Allie. I don't mind, but like I said, it's already taken care of."

As they walk back to Ms. Allie's office, she begins to ask AJ what college he would like to attend. He explains to her that he was considering not going for a while, but now that his situation has changed, he would like to attend the University of Arkansas at Pine Bluff.

"That's a great university, and several of our graduates this year are planning on attending," Ms. Allie responds.

"I know—two of my friends are going. We are planning on leaving the same day and heading up there together."

"That's great. You guys will love it there. You are this year's salutatorian, right?"

"Yes ma'am."

"Have you written your speech for the graduation ceremony yet?"

"Yes ma'am. Connie made sure I did. She helped me with it last night."

"You and Connie are very close, I see."

"Yes, we are. She's been a real friend through all of this I've been dealing with."

"That's what a friend is supposed to do—be there for you no matter what and help you when you need a shoulder to lean on."

"She has definitely been there for me."

Ms. Allie stops in front of a closed door. "Okay, here we are—my office. Now before we go in, are you sure you don't mind talking with the officer in the room?"

"Ms. Allie, it's okay. I don't mind."

"I just want to be sure."

"I didn't want to talk about my situation at first, but Connie helped me to see that maybe I needed to talk to someone before things got a lot worse, and yesterday they almost did. I should have said something long ago."

Ms. Allie smiles gently. "Well, I, for one, am glad she convinced you to talk to me. Whatever is going on, the principal, the school officer, the teachers, and I are here to help every student however we can. We just need you guys to trust us and come to us when you have a problem, no matter what it is."

"Thanks, I needed to hear that."

"Are you ready to go in and talk about this fully?"

"Yes ma'am, I think I am."

"Okay." Ms. Allie opens the door and leads AJ into her office, where the school officer is waiting. "Mr. Williams, this is Anthony Harris, and he is here to talk about the incident that happened yesterday morning."

The officer nods politely to AJ as he and Ms. Allie each take a seat. "Hi, son. How are you doing today?" Officer Williams asks.

"I'm doing a lot better than yesterday."

"If you don't mind me asking, what happened to you yesterday?"

AJ clears his throat. "As I was telling Ms. Allie, the problem has been taken care of, but what happened yesterday, to be honest, had nothing to do with be being jumped. I lied about that 'cause I didn't want to cause any trouble for my mom."

"Did your mom do this to you?"

"Oh, *no* sir, but if I would have told what happened, she would have probably shot my dad."

"You mean to tell us that your father did that to you?" Officer Williams clarifies.

"Yes sir, but this was the first time he hit me. I usually just get cursed at. My mom gets beat on all the time."

"How long has this been going on, son?"

AJ shrugs. "He's been beating on my mom for some time. A couple days ago we moved in with my mom's friend, but I had to go to my house and get those papers for you"—he glances at Ms. Allie—"yesterday, and that's when he started wailing on me."

"Why didn't you ever go to someone for help, son?"

AJ looks down at his fidgety hands. "I was ashamed, and he made it seem like it was our fault and that we deserved it. He got arrested once for breaking my mom's jaw some time ago, but he wasn't locked up very long, and when he got out, he came back. The courts let him come back after a slap on the wrist. So if the courts wouldn't keep him away, he was free to do whatever he wanted to us, and he would laugh and make jokes every time my mom would say she was calling the police. Saying stuff like 'Go ahead, call them. I could use a week or two away from you and that boy.'"

Officer Williams leans forward in his seat. "Anthony, you say the problem is handled now. What did you mean by that?"

"Well, yesterday he showed up at the hospital, and he and my mom got into an argument when she found out what he did to me. When he tried to hit her, she pulled out her gun."

"Did she shoot him?"

"Almost, but thankfully I made it out there before she did, and I talked her into putting the gun away. Hospital security had called the police, and some guy recorded the whole thing, so with the video and everyone that witnessed it all, the police said we won't have to fear him for a while."

Ms. Allie speaks up. "That's a good start to regaining your sense of self-worth, but I think you and your mom will need to have some type of counseling so that the both of you can start to heal from this ordeal."

"Ms. Allie, thank you, but I think we will be okay now that he is gone, and we are staying with my mom's friend."

Officer Williams says, "She's right, you know. I see a lot of these situations, and those that seek help through means other than family tend to be able to put the pieces of their lives back together a little easier than those who don't."

"We don't have money for something like that. He was the only one working."

"Son, there are options and programs that don't cost you or your mom a thing, and they help you guys with whatever y'all would need. Here, take this card." Officer Williams pulls out his wallet and slides a card out of it. "My friend works for the Domestic Violence and Child Advocacy Center. Promise me you or your mom will reach out to her soon. I'm sure she can help you guys."

"Officer Williams, Ms. Allie, thanks. I'll be sure to give my mom this card and have her call. For now, I'm ready to try and put it behind us and move on."

"Son, with something like this, it's not that simple to just move on."

"I understand, Officer Williams. I just meant that I want to focus more on graduation and giving my speech. Connie and I stayed up all night getting it right, and I want this speech to be how I'm remembered here—not as the kid that got beat up by his dad."

Ms. Allie responds, "Mr. Harris, with all that you have accomplished here at this school, I believe that is far from how we will remember you."

"Thank you, Ms. Allie, for saying that. If there is nothing else, ma'am, I should be heading to class."

"Okay, Anthony, but do me a favor—remember that we, meaning any of the school staff, are here to help in any way that we can and that you or any other student can come to us with any problem."

"Yes ma'am. I'll remember that from now on."

As AJ heads to his class, he reaches in his pocket and pulls out the card Officer Williams gave him. Maybe it would be a good idea to call, if only for some insight to the legal system pertaining to domestic violence. He turns down the hall to his class and sees that Connie is standing there, waiting for him.

She walks up to him. "Well, sir?"

"Well what?" AJ responds.

"What did she say?"

"Nothing too much. Just wanted to know what happened."

"And?"

"And what?"

Connie sighs. "What did you tell her?"

"I told them everything."

"Who else was in there?"

"Officer Williams."

"What did he say?"

Now it's AJ's turn to sigh. "Con, shouldn't you be in class?"

"Boy, don't try and change the subject. Now, I asked, what did he say?"

"Con, you do know I have a mom already, right?"

"What are you trying to say?"

"You know what—let's just get to class."

"Not till you explain that last statement," Connie pushes the point.

AJ tries to walk past Connie, and she thumps him on his forehead. "Ouch, girl. Watch it with those nails."

"It's not the nails you gonna have to worry about if you keep getting smart with me."

"There you go with them violent tendencies. Anyway, he gave me a card to reach out to someone he knows at the Domestic Violence and Child Advocacy Center."

"But are you gonna use it?"

"I'm thinking about calling, but I think my mom is the one that needs to."

"AJ, it really doesn't matter who calls as long as one of y'all do."

AJ and Connie begin to walk to class just as the principal rounds the corner.

He stops in front of them. "Ms. Smalls and Mr. Harris, why are we not in class yet?"

AJ responds, "Sorry, Mr. Anderson. We just left Ms. Allie's office. We are heading to class now."

"Hurry up and get there. I can't have two of my ace students hanging in the halls and being late to class. Gotta be an example for the others."

"Yes sir!" AJ says.

"And congratulations to both of you. Keep up the good work. And, Anthony, I'm looking forward to hearing your speech come graduation day."

"Thank you, Mr. Anderson."

As AJ and Connie walk into class late, everyone turns and stares at the pair of them. All at once, everyone stands up and beings to clap and embrace AJ. AJ is somewhat in shock, taken aback because he didn't realize how many people cared for him—not just as a member of their graduating class, but also as a friend. The teacher invites AJ to share what's going on, but only if he is comfortable. After just sharing with Ms. Allie and Officer Williams, AJ isn't feeling as hesitant as he previously was. AJ stands in front of the class and thanks everyone. Then he proceeds to explain what is going on in his life. Everyone is quiet as AJ tells the horrible truth of his life leading up to yesterday's events. Every so often, someone gasps as if they can't believe what they are hearing. When AJ finishes his story with what happened yesterday, one by one, multiple students stand up and begin a dialogue of the horrors they have dealt with over the years.

As his classmates share more and more of their lives, AJ doesn't feel so ashamed or alone anymore. For the rest of that class period, Ms. Hicks leaves the floor open to anyone who wants to discuss the topic of domestic violence and how it affects not just those it's happening to but also those people who care about you.

One student stands up and talks about how one night his dad came in drunk and just began ripping into him. His dad had gotten into a fight and had been beat up. With a shrug, the student says he guesses his dad wanted revenge but knew going back to face the guy who'd beat him up was not a good idea. Each time his dad would come in drunk and attack him, he would just take it, because if he was getting the beating, that meant his mom and little brother were safe.

Just as another student stands up to tell her story, the bell rings to switch classes, but no one wants to leave. Ms. Hicks assures them that they can pick up the conversation tomorrow. As everyone starts gathering their things for the next class, AJ walks row to row, thanking his fellow classmates for their compassion and understanding.

Connie waits for AJ out in the hall as he stops to talk to Ms. Hicks for a moment. Although Connie can't hear what's being said, she is sure of one thing: her friend will be all right now that he knows that not only she, Ms. Allie, and Officer Williams are in his corner, but so is the whole school. As Connie stands there, waiting on AJ, she begins to think of all the students who have been going through the same thing but were afraid to speak up until now. What could be done to spread the word far and loud enough so that everyone knows that domestic violence has to stop? Then she remembers that the drama class does a theater production every year during the summer . . . why not ask to do a play geared toward that very subject? In light of recent events, she is sure that almost everyone would be on board, but she also knows there will be some who won't think that a school play is a great way of dealing with such a touchy subject. However, once Connie gets an idea in her head, she is determined to see it through, especially when it's something she feels needs to be said and when everyone shies away from it as if to say, "It's not happening to me, so it's not my problem."

AJ finishes talking with Ms. Hicks and is surprised to see Connie still standing in the hall, waiting for him.

"Con, what are you still doing out here? Remember what Mr. Anderson said. We gotta set an example for the other students. You can't be just standing out here in the hall."

"Boy, I was waiting on your slow tail."

"What? You don't think I know my way to my next class?"

"Boy, hush. Anyway, I wanted to talk to you about something I had in mind." They begin to walk toward their next classes.

"Okay, Con. What is it this time that your mind has thought up?"

"Well, if you really want to know, I was wondering what you guys are doing for the summer theater production. Although you will be graduated, you are still going to participate, right?"

"Yes, I am, but I have no clue what we are doing right now. Why? Are you planning on helping out this year?"

"Um, no, but I do have something in mind."

"Okay, well you know Ms. Hawkins is open for ideas, but whoever's idea gets picked has to help in some way. So are you sure you want to do whatever it is you are thinking about?"

"Can you ask for me?"

"Nope. Your idea—you ask."

"Really? You can't ask for me?"

"Nope, not gonna do it. Now we better get to class before we get busted again."

She looks over at him with puppy-dog eyes and says, "Please? I would do it for you."

AJ responds with, "Sorry, no can do, and can you stop looking at me like somebody stole your dog? 'Cause it's not working."

Connie pinches his arm.

"Ouch! What was that for?"

"'Cause you won't ask her for me."

"Really, Con, and your first thought was to pinch me for that?"

"Yep, and I'll do it again if you don't like it."

"Girl, you play too much. Now come on here before we are late for class."

"So you really not gonna ask?" Connie persists.

"Okay, Con . . . after school, tell me what you have in mind, and if it sounds good, I'll consider asking Ms. Hawkins if we may be able to do it. Just remember, Con—if she goes for it, you have to help put it together or even be in it."

CHAPTER SIX

JAMES MADISON HIGH SCHOOL
THE SAME DAY

Later that day, AJ meets back up with Connie outside of school to discuss her ideas for the summer theater production.

"Okay, Con, now what was your lil' mind thinking about doing for the summer play?"

Connie plops down on a bench. "Well, AJ, I was thinking of you guys not doing a *play* this time, but instead doing several performances that have a story to tell. Like little skits that have to do with domestic violence, but we use poetry to tell the stories."

"Really, Con, that's your idea?"

"Yes . . ."

"No, Con. Not gonna happen. Not gonna ask about doing that."

"Why? What's wrong with that?" She folds her arms and stares at him defensively.

"First off, Con, the drama team has been doing plays in the summer at the Children's Medical Center—key word, *children*."

"What if we could do it at a different place this year?"

"Con, you do know you said *we*, right?"

"Yes, I know what I said."

"So you are making a commitment to this if I ask Ms. Hawkins and if she agrees to do it?"

"Yes, AJ!"

AJ dwells on the idea for a moment, then responds, "Okay, Con, let's go."

"Go where?"

"Let's go talk to Ms. Hawkins."

Connie raises her eyebrows. "Wait, *what*?"

"I said I would ask, but you have to explain your idea to her."

"Since you are already participating, why can't we just say it's your idea?"

"'Cause it's not. That's why."

"Oh, we getting a smart mouth now."

AJ nods. "Yep, now it's my turn to have the upper hand."

"You can have the upper hand, but if you keep getting smart with me, I'mma send you to the upper room."

"See, Con, there you go with them violent thoughts again."

"Boy, hush. Ain't nobody gonna do nothin' to you, so stop your whining, and let's go." She stands up and stomps back toward the school.

As they're heading toward the doors of the school, they see Ms. Hawkins walking to her car. AJ and Connie hurry to intercept the teacher.

"Hi, Ms. Hawkins," Connie says.

The teacher turns to the kids. "Hi, Ms. Smalls, Mr. Harris."

AJ says, "Ms. Hawkins, are you in a hurry? 'Cause Connie and I have a question to ask you."

Ms. Hawkins leans against her car. "Sure, guys. What can I help with?"

"Well, we were wondering what you had planned for the drama class this summer."

"To be honest, I haven't figured it out yet. Why do you ask?"

AJ gestures to his friend. "Connie has an idea she wanted to run by you."

Ms. Hawkins smiles, welcoming the idea. "Okay, what is the idea that you have in mind, Ms. Smalls?"

"Well, Ms. Hawkins, I'm sure you've heard by now about what happened to AJ yesterday."

Ms. Hawkins nods, a grimace on her face now. "Yes, I have, and I'm sorry that you had to endure such troubled times."

AJ responds, "It's been rough, but we made it through, ma'am."

"Now, Ms. Smalls, what were you thinking? I'm open to any and all suggestions at the moment."

"Well, Ms. Hawkins, I was thinking that instead of putting on a play this year, maybe we could put on a show like they did in the movie *Honey*, but change it up a bit, and direct it toward stopping domestic violence by using poetry, dance, and skits to tell different stories, and we know a great poet that can write beautiful poetry."

"Oh, really, do we now? This is sounding good so far, Ms. Smalls. However, there is a big problem—the Children's Medical Center has a strict policy about no productions that have to do with adult topics or violence."

Connie nods. "AJ told me about that. I'm certain that my dad would ask a good friend of his about us using his theater if I just asked him."

"Well, Ms. Smalls, it seems you are on top of the ball. Where is this theater located?"

"It's the Majestic Theatre downtown."

"And who is this poet that we know?"

"You're looking at him!" Connie inclines her head toward AJ.

Ms. Hawkins turns her attention to him. "Anthony, I didn't know you wrote poetry."

A little caught off guard, AJ replies, "Yes ma'am, I do, and I told Con it's for my own comfort." He gives the side-eye to Connie.

Ms. Hawkins takes a moment to think on the idea, and then she asks, "Okay, can you write one tonight that's like a conversation piece between a husband and wife?"

AJ purses his lips together, thinking. "I think I know what you mean, Ms. Hawkins."

"Okay, you two work on that tonight, and I'll look it over tomorrow, and if it fits the vision I have in mind, we will get started on putting something together."

"I think I have a good one in mind, but if it's good enough, Con, you will have to read it with me."

"You mean on stage?" Connie asks quickly.

"*Yes*, on stage."

"Um . . . no. I'll do my part by getting the theater," Connie replies.

Ms. Hawkins speaks up. "Sorry, Ms. Smalls, but Anthony is correct—if your idea is picked, you have to be in it. Meaning,

Ms. Smalls, that you have to be on stage in some fashion. Are you willing to do that?"

AJ reassures her, "Don't worry, Con, I have something in mind that I'm sure you wouldn't mind doing. I wrote a poem that we can read back and forth, and we can have a performance going on that goes along with the poem. All you have to do is stand to the side and read."

"AJ, are you sure that's all I have to do?"

"Yes, Con. That's all."

She hesitates, then says, "Okay, I'm in."

Ms. Hawkins smiles. "Great! You guys be prepared to work hard on putting together a great show, just like they did in the movie *Honey*," Ms. Hawkins says as she turns to get in her car.

As the kids turn to walk to Connie's car, Connie says, "Okay, AJ, whatever this poem is, it better be just as good as the other ones, or you know what's going to happen."

"Yeah, I know, you gonna make me write it over."

"Yeah, and then I'mma kick your ass."

"Damn, Con. Does everything lead up to you wanting to hit me?"

She shrugs casually. "Pretty much, yeah, it does." They slide into her car, and she pulls out of the school parking lot.

"Well, Con, this poem is pretty good. I read it at an open mic a while back, and it was well received. It's called 'Reality Check.' You'll like it, I promise."

"We will see, Mr. Bony Butt."

"Really, Con? You gonna start that again?"

Connie smirks. "Yepper, and there is nothing you can do about it."

"Girl, just come by the house later and see for yourself. I'll have it typed up by dinnertime."

"If Darlene is cooking dinner, I'll be there before then. I'm not missing out on her cooking—not after all that good cookin' she did yesterday. What was in that banana pudding? I could have ate that all by myself."

"Con, you lucky I gave you some. I normally don't share when it comes to banana puddin'."

"Well, next time I'll ask her to make me my own batch, and I won't share with you—how 'bout that?"

"How about you just come by and read this poem with me in front of my mom and Aunt Darlene? Then we will know if it's good enough to show Ms. Hawkins or if it needs to be reworked."

"I'll be there around six or seven, okay?" She pulls into Darlene's driveway to drop AJ off.

"Aight, cool. See you then."

***

As soon as AJ walks into Darlene's house, he tells his mom and Darlene that after dinner, he and Connie want them to hear something he wrote, but he doesn't say what it is.

He heads up to his room and begins to type out his poem, and just as he does, his phone rings. It's Connie calling with news that she just talked to Chris, a freshman at school who writes poetry, and she told him what was happening with the summer theater performance. He wants to be in on the project.

"Cool," AJ responds. "If he can come, bring him over with you. But Con, I don't know how good of a poet he is, so until I read some of his work, he can't have any banana puddin'."

She laughs. "Boy, hush. You didn't know how good you was till I told you."

"Okay, Con, jeez. I was just joking. No need to get all defensive."

"Anyway, boy, he already in the car with me, and we are on our way."

AJ glances at the clock. It's barely five o'clock. "Girl, we decided on six or seven."

"I'm coming now. Want to make somethin' of it?"

"There you go again, Con. You need some anger management, 'cause you have issues."

"My only issue is kicking your tail when you get out of line. And if you say 'what line,' be ready to get smacked upside your head when I get there."

"Jeez, girl. Calm down with your bipolar self. I'm about to type this poem up, so I'll see you guys when you get here, okay?"

"Bye, Mr. Bony Butt. See you in a few."

AJ hangs up the phone, shakes his head, and thinks that this girl is crazy, but she is his kind of crazy. He lets out a slight laugh.

For the second time, AJ begins to type, but he turns his phone off and locks his door first so he won't get disturbed again.

Reality Check

Anthony: My hands were made for strength,
         Yet I have used them to torment . . .

Connie: I was there when all seemed lost.
         I was there when no one seemed to care.

I was there when you fell to your knees
And prayed, and yet you treated me with such
Disgrace . . .

Anthony: No words now nor then could explain my actions,
Yet through it all you stood the pain.
The mental and physical abuse that
You withstood couldn't be seen through
My eyes, yet you stood by my side . . .

Connie: I was there holding your hand when
People shunned you; I cared for you,
I shared with you, I even cried for you . . .

Anthony: Through the years my words have been
Hurtful and my fist forceful.
You deserve more than I; you trusted me
As your husband to keep you safe, yet
I have harmed you in every way . . .

Connie: No more of your lies, no more of your cries,
No more pain, and no more scared nights.
You were my husband, and I said till death
Do us part, but I deserved more . . .

Anthony: Now that I sit in this cell with my hands
Covering my face, my charges read
Murder one, no bail.
You deserved more than I . . .

Connie: As I lie here with my arms crossed

And a rose placed over my heart,

As my children weep and the preacher speaks,

My body is lowered where I will forever

Rest in peace

Why?

Together: This is just a poem, but to many it should be

A reality check . . .

Just as AJ finishes typing up his poem, he hears the doorbell ring. "Must be Connie and Chris. Let me get down there and see what this dude is all about," AJ thinks to himself. As he heads down the stairs, he hears Connie talking with Darlene about her banana pudding. He hurries to the kitchen before Connie can finish asking if there is any left.

He interrupts, "Con, what are you in here bugging my aunt about? And it better not be what I think it's about, 'cause it's all gone. I ate it all, so you can stop asking."

"Boy, please. Who are you talking to like that? You must have lost your mind."

Darlene lets out a slight laugh and excuses herself. "I'll see y'all later, and I might make more pudding for dessert after dinner." On her way out of the kitchen, she taps AJ on his shoulder and says, "Be careful—she's got your number."

AJ looks back over to Connie and asks, "So where is this guy Chris you were bringing with you?"

She points to the other room. "He's in the living room, writing something."

They head out of the kitchen to join Chris in the living room, and as soon as AJ sees him, he steps back and grabs Connie by the arm to stop her. "That big ole dude is a *freshman*?"

"Yes," Connie replies, "Now let go of my arm, and don't be rude."

AJ mumbles under his breath, "Looks like he needs to be a linebacker in the NFL instead of writing poetry."

Connie replies, "I heard that!"

Then Chris speaks up. "I heard that too. But don't worry—I get that a lot. People say that to me every day, and I have to tell them I don't even like sports. See that look on your face right now—it's the same look everybody makes." He stands up and extends a hand. "Anyway, man, I'm Chris. Connie told me what you guys were doing instead of a play this summer, and I wanted to take part in it. I heard what happened to you, and I've lived a similar life, only my mom didn't make it out."

AJ shakes Chris's hand, and then they sit on the couch. "I'm sorry to hear that, man, and I'm sorry about the linebacker thing a minute ago. How did you ever get past something like that?"

Chris inhales deeply. "I didn't, and I don't think I ever will. It's a challenge every day, but my poetry helps."

AJ nods, relating to that thought. "When did you start writing?"

"Shortly after my mom died. My aunt and I started going to counseling, and this counselor suggested I write down my feelings, and we could talk about them each time I visited."

"So going there helped you deal with everything?"

"Let's just say if I hadn't gone, I wouldn't be here today. Writing down how I felt led to writing poetry."

"Man, that's pretty much how I started."

"I was writing one that deals with domestic violence a few minutes ago before the linebacker thing, if you care to read it."

"That's cool, but I tell you what—after dinner, I have something set up, kind of a dry run over something I wrote for me and Con to read on stage if everything goes right. If it's okay with your aunt, why don't you stay over with Con for dinner? Then after, we can read the poems to my aunt and mom and gauge how they react before showing them to Ms. Hawkins tomorrow."

"I'm sure my aunt won't mind, but do you think your aunt will cook enough for one more mouth?" asks Chris.

AJ laughs. "Hey, Con, you think my aunt gonna cook enough for him to join us for dinner?"

"I'm not gonna answer that. Let's just let him see for himself."

After an hour or so, dinner is ready, and everyone is pretty hungry by then. Chris gapes at the sheer quantity of the food. "Wow, dude. Your aunt really cooked a lot! Does she cook like this all the time?"

"Yepper, it's her thing. She cooks enough for the guys down at the park and anyone that don't have much to eat."

"Oh, okay, I see. It sure smells good."

"Yeah, just wait till you taste her greens and potatoes."

"Can't wait, man!"

"Let's go wash up before we eat," AJ suggests. As they head off to wash up, Chris asks how his speech for graduation is going. "It's finished. Con helped me write it last night, and I'm glad too. With graduation a few weeks away, it was stressful trying to figure out just what to say."

"Yeah, I bet, man. I can't wait till it's my turn to walk across that stage."

"Let's head back to the table before Con gets ahold of my banana puddin'," suggests AJ.

"Man, what is it about that banana puddin'?"

"You'll see if you get to taste it." AJ laughs.

When the guys make it back to the table, everyone sits down and enjoys a satisfying home-cooked meal.

Afterward, Chris says, "Oh man, I'm stuffed."

"You should be! You ate three plates!" Connie exclaims.

Chris defends himself, "Hey, I'm still growing, and so is my appetite." Everyone chuckles as Chris rubs his belly. "That was really good. Can I take a plate home with me?"

"Sure!" Darlene replies. "And thanks for the compliment."

Janice speaks up. "Now, Anthony, what is it you wanted us to hear?"

"Well, if Con would help me with this, we will read it shortly."

Connie responds, "I'll help if you share your puddin'."

"Oh, girl, I made one just for you 'cause you know Anthony's not gonna share," Darlene states.

AJ says, "Also, Mom, Chris has written one, too, that he's going to read."

"Okay then, let's go in the family room, 'cause I really want to hear this," Janice says.

As everyone enters the family room, Janice, Darlene, and Chris sit while AJ and Connie stand in front of the fireplace.

Connie whispers to him, "I'm nervous."

AJ replies, "Then it's a good thing we doing it here first." He looks over to his mom and says, "This is a poem, but it's a conversation piece. It's called 'Reality Check.'"

Janice looks over to Darlene with a look of wonder as if to say, "How can it be both a poem and a conversation?" But then AJ starts to read, and Connie follows his lead. By the end of the poem, both Darlene and Janice sit there with tears in their eyes and their hands covering their mouths. Chris turns his head and wipes his eyes discretely, trying to hide the fact that he is crying too.

Janice gets up and hugs AJ and Connie while tears run down her face.

Darlene can only say "Wow" while wiping tears from her eyes. Chris also gets up and hugs AJ and Connie.

Chris says, "I don't know if I can follow that, but I'll try." Everyone takes a seat and is very attentive as Chris prepares to read his poem. He looks over at everyone and says, "I hope you guys like this poem. It's called 'Addiction.' Okay, here goes."

Addiction

I remember the days your liquor spoke

    Louder than your words.

Your head was bottled up full of a

    180-proof killer.

Matched the undeniable ego of your

    Absinthe rectified spirit.

There was once a time I believed in a

    Thin line between addiction and abuse.

But my black-and-blue vision blurred

    The very beginnings of a silver lining

With the break of the clouds
        That was my mortality.

Your lips slurred my name like the indictment
        On the tip of my tongue I bit
To save a life.

A hesitation of a solemn attestation
        To the truth I bear.

Introspective thoughts on an external
        Observation.

In your head lay a mental state of affairs.
        I chide myself in defense
Of your savagery that molested my soul
        Into silence.

Because my black-and-blue vision blurred
        The very beginnings of a silver lining
With the break of the clouds
        That was my own mortality.

In which I find myself a Stockholm victim.

Your abuse became my addiction.

Morose, morose.

I remember the days your liquor spoke

    Louder than your words . . .

Everyone stands up and gives Chris a hug, thanking him for sharing what, for him, is a very emotional poem. AJ is hesitant at first to say anything, but he admits that Chris is a talented writer and that he would be proud to work with him on the theater project.

Connie asks, "Okay, so does this mean we are ready to present these poems to Ms. Hawkins in the morning?"

AJ responds, "Yes, Con. Then all we have to do is wait and see if she okays the performance."

Darlene speaks up and says, "You guys don't have anything to worry about. I'm sure Ms. Hawkins will want to put this in her production."

AJ explains, "The entire performance is based on stopping domestic violence, and it's Con's brainchild."

Chris adds, "A lot of my friends know what happened with my mom, and if I mention to them what we are trying to do, I know they will want to help."

"That would be great," says AJ. "We are going to need dancers, singers, poets, actors—"

"Wait, AJ. This is going to be a huge production. Are you sure we will have time for something this big?" Connie asks.

"Oh no, you are not backing out now," AJ states firmly, giving Connie the side-eye.

"I'm not backing out," she hastily adds. "I'm just saying that with graduation so close, do we have the time right now to focus on something so big?"

"Con, don't worry. We have plenty of time to work on it after graduation. The performance isn't till the end of summer, remember?"

Chris stands up. "Well, guys, I'm going to head home to write some more. Ms. Darlene and Ms. Janice, thank you for a nice dinner, and AJ, I'll see you at school tomorrow."

Janice says, "Thank you, Chris, for sharing your poetry with us."

"Chris, wait. I'll give you a ride home," Connie says, jumping up.

***

That night, Chris uploads a video he took of AJ and Connie performing AJ's poem. He links it to his Wattpad account and announces to his followers that pending approval from the theater teacher, this year's performance is aimed at stopping domestic violence. He adds that dancers, actors, poets, and singers are needed.

***

The next morning, before AJ, Connie, and Chris can speak with Ms. Hawkins about the poems they wrote, there are at least twenty to thirty students lined up at her office to sign up to perform in any aspect that they can. Ms. Hawkins is astounded at how many students have come to offer their talents.

When Connie and AJ question how everyone already knows about the show, Chris says "I'm sorry, guys, but I recorded you guys last night and posted a link to the video in my poetry collection on Wattpad. I didn't expect this many people to see it and respond."

AJ clasps his hand on Chris's shoulder. "No need to be sorry, bro. Besides, I did say we needed more people, and boy, did you come through."

Ms. Hawkins steps out of her office and calls AJ, Connie, and Chris into her room.

"It seems as though the word has gotten out about the theater production for this year," she says, "and I have to say I'm surprised. We have not only our regular students participating this year, but also some new faces. So, Ms. Smalls, I think you had a great idea, and we are going to put on an amazing show. This year, however, we are going to do something a little different. Instead of the money from tickets going to the drama class, we will be donating all proceeds to the Domestic Violence and Child Advocacy Center. I hope you guys are ready to work hard and campaign for this show to be a success. Also, it will be up to you guys to sign everyone up and get to know their talents. So with that being said, congratulations. We have a production to put together, but for now, you two, Anthony and Connie, have a very important day coming up. We will continue this preparation after graduation. It seems as though I, on the other hand, have a lot of work to start on right now to get this production approved."

CHAPTER SEVEN

DARLENE'S HOME
THE NIGHT BEFORE GRADUATION

"**H**ey, AJ, are you awake?"

"I am now, Con," AJ says groggily into the phone. "What's up?"

"I couldn't sleep, so I've been up pacing all night."

"Con, it's four in the morning. You better get some sleep 'cause you know we have a full day ahead of us."

"Okay, I'll try."

"Good night, Con. I'm going back to sleep."

***

Three hours later, AJ's phone rings again.

"Con, what is it now? I'm trying to sleep."

"Boy, get your butt up. It's seven o'clock, and I'm on my way to Darlene's house."

"Con, have you been to sleep yet?" AJ stumbles out of bed and digs through his clothes, holding the phone between his cheek and shoulder.

"Nope, not a wink."

"*Really*, Con?"

"Boy, you can't talk. You stay up all night all the time."

"Yeah, but I don't drive after. There's a big difference."

"Boy, hush, and get yourself together. We have a lot to do before graduation starts."

"Yeah, I know. I'm up and almost ready." He pulls on his clothes for the day.

"Hurry up. I'm about to pull up."

"Okay, I just need to brush my teeth."

"Yeah, do that, 'cause I don't need no funky breath blowing in my face." She hangs up abruptly.

After brushing his teeth, AJ grabs a slice of toast and kisses his mom on his way out the door. He then turns around and reminds his mom the ceremony starts at two o'clock.

She replies, "Darlene and I will be there at one so we can get good seats right up front." She grins with excitement.

AJ rushes out of the house to Connie's car, and just as he is about to get in, Connie asks, "Are you forgetting something, sir?"

"Nope, I got everything I need. Got my speech right here. My phone. My suit. Nope, not forgetting anything."

"Okay, well what about your cap and gown?" Connie sarcastically asks.

AJ covers his mouth with his hand in shame. "Oh, yeah. Can't forget that."

"Yeah, Mr. Forgetful."

"Hey, I'll take that name over bony butt any day."

"Boy, just go get your cap and gown so we can go."

Just as AJ steps out of the car, his mom brings his forgotten items out to him.

"Thanks, Mom."

"I figured you might need these, son." She laughs.

As Connie and AJ head off to the stadium to prepare for graduation, Janice heads back in the house with the biggest smile she's had in years. When she gets back inside, Darlene asks, "Why are you smiling so big? Did you sneak off last night to go get you a Bob?"

"No, nasty. I'm smiling 'cause my son graduates today."

"Ohh, okay. I'm just asking 'cause Bob makes me smile just like that. And, by the way, it's *Ms.* Nasty."

"Darlene girl, I'm not talking to you anymore. I'm about to make me some breakfast and get ready to go watch my baby walk across that stage."

"You mean *our* baby, don't you? He's just like a son to me too, you know."

"All right, Darlene—our baby. Now shouldn't you go get ready too?"

"Oh girl, it don't take me long to get ready."

"What takes me so long is deciding which wig to put on."

"Girl, you are too throwed."

"Yes, I am, and you are my best friend, so that makes you just as throwed.

***

About half an hour after noon, parents begin to arrive outside the stadium and search for their children to take pictures before the graduation ceremony begins. After Darlene and Janice locate Connie and AJ, AJ hears someone calling his name.

It is Officer Williams, the school's duty officer. He walks over to them. "I'm sorry to interrupt you guys, but may I speak with you and your mother in private?"

"Yes sir, Officer Williams," AJ says, stepping aside. "What's going on?"

"I wanted to let you guys know that your father was seen on property."

AJ recoils. "Wait, what? I thought he was still in jail." His voice rises in anger. "How could he be out already?"

"I don't have an answer for that, and since he has a ticket and hasn't caused any problems, our hands are tied. However, it's your graduation, and you, Mrs. Harris, have a no-contact order against him, right? If he comes within fifty feet of either of you, then we can have him escorted off-site and rearrested."

AJ glances at his mother. "Mom, are you okay? If you want to leave, we can. They can always mail my diploma to me."

Although her hands shake slightly as she takes AJ's hands in hers, she insists, "No, son. This is your day. You have worked so hard for it, and I refuse to let your father take this day from either of us. Officer Williams, thank you for letting us know he's here."

He dips his head. "You are welcome, ma'am. We will do our best to make sure that he stays away from you guys. Don't worry—my people have their eyes on him. Any sudden moves, and we are there."

***

Half an hour later, everyone starts to head into the stadium to take their seats. Still outside, AJ notices his dad standing out near his car.

"Mom, you guys go in and take your seats, and I'll be in shortly. I have something I need to take care of."

"Okay, son, but hurry in. The ceremony is starting soon."

"I know, Mom. This won't take long. I promise." AJ then turns and heads toward his father. The closer he gets to his father, the more nervous he feels—the sweatier his hands get, and the harder his heart pounds. Now standing face to face once again with the man who has brought so much torment, anger, and despair to his life, AJ only wants to know why he has come to his graduation.

"I thought you were still in jail," AJ mutters.

"I was. I made bail this morning, pending trial. I didn't come to cause any trouble. I just wanted to see you graduate."

"You don't deserve to see any part of this!" AJ raises his voice.

"I know I don't, and I know you don't want me here."

"If you know that, then why did you come? To torment Mom again by letting her see that you are out again?"

"No, son . . . I only came to see you graduate. I promise I didn't want to upset you or your mom. That's why I'm still standing out here, waiting till everyone goes inside, and then I was going to slip in and sit in the back."

"I prefer if you didn't, 'cause as you said, I don't want you here."

His father hangs his head. "Okay, I'll leave, but I am proud of you, and I am truly sorry for everything."

"You say that now, but where was the *sorry* when you first got angry and yelled at Mom? Where was the *sorry* when you knew you was wrong? You know what, man? I don't get it—what happened to the man Mom married? What happened to the man that wrote Mom poetry?" He glances back toward the stadium. "My graduation is about to start, and I hope you respect my wishes and don't come in. But do me a favor, and think about what I just asked about the old you."

"Okay, son, I will respect that."

Just as AJ heads back up the stairs toward the stadium entrance, his dad calls out to him, "Hey, Anthony!"

AJ stops but doesn't turn around. "Yeah? What?"

"Son, I did take your advice from the last time we talked. I joined AA and signed up for anger-management classes."

AJ takes a deep breath. "Good for you!" he yells as he starts walking up the stairs again.

He makes it into the stadium just as teachers are making sure each student is in his or her correct spot in line.

Connie rushes over, asking, "Where did you disappear to?"

"I had something to do, but it's handled now, so let's graduate, okay?"

As the students file into the center of the stadium, everyone stands up and applauds, not only for their own kids but for every kid graduating that day. After all the students are at their seats, everyone remains standing for the Pledge of Allegiance.

The graduating ceremony finally begins, and as the master of ceremonies stands at the podium, Connie turns in her seat to face AJ, who is sitting behind her, and whispers, "Are you ready to give your speech? You will be going up there in about thirty minutes."

"Yes, Con, I'm ready," AJ responds with confidence.

"Okay, 'cause I can't go up there and hold your hand."

"Really, Con? Still with the jokes."

Not long after, the master of ceremonies announces, "Parents, friends, and esteemed colleagues, please stand and welcome this year's class salutatorian, Mr. Anthony Harris."

AJ swallows and tries to dismiss any lingering nervousness as he steps onto the stage. He takes his spot in front of the mic. "Good evening," he begins. "It is indeed an honor to stand before you this afternoon to address the 2016 graduating class of the *great* James Madison High School. I am Anthony Harris, your class salutatorian. As a child, I was fortunate enough to have a mother that believed that I could be more than what I can see. The road here was not an easy one, as there were many times that I did not want to continue on, especially when things seemed to be unbearable and unbeatable.

"I want to take our graduating class back to our freshman year in the fall of 2011. We came in with only ourselves and no knowledge of what would be, not knowing any of the obstacles we would face. Over the last few years, we have trod through so much. We have laughed till it hurt; we have cried till we couldn't cry anymore; we have overslept. We have survived on less than four hours of sleep, crammed for tests, and dealt with social problems, and some of us were even on the verge of not being here today.

"We were told that since we went to Madison, we would not make it. People talked down about our school, dehumanized us for attending, and found every negative thing they could about the *great* James Madison. They tried defining us by statistics! Through all of that, I have to say that even though sometimes bad things happen to us, *we are still here*!

"So what makes Madison *great*? Could it be a 2015 district championship football team? A multi-award-winning band? A defending champion basketball team? Or even an award-winning theater project? Or is it the teachers who learned our names and showed they care?

"Class of 2016, we may be from the smallest school in the Dallas Independent School District. We may be the smallest graduating class, but I want every one of you to look at who is around you in their green caps and gowns. You may have had problems with them, they may be your best friend, or you may not know them at all. Put all that aside, shake their hand, give them a hug, show them some love. Tell them you are proud of them.

"Now, parents, look around at not only your family, but also the other families here. If it were not for the love and dedication that you all put in, this evening would not have been possible. I want to thank every last one of you for your contributions. If no one caught the point of this speech, I want to say to the class of 2016 . . . when others doubt you . . . push harder. When other say you are from the bottom . . . remind them it's the bottom that holds you up. When others put you down . . . walk with your head up high. When others scandalize your name . . . speak good things about them. When others say you are weak . . . show them your strength. When others say you will never make it . . . invite them to your celebrations.

"Graduates . . . be strong . . . stay ready . . . be who you were meant to be, and stay focused. Class of 2016, congratulations! We made it!"

ABOUT THE AUTHOR

Anthony Harris, born December 22, 1976, to Janice Harris as the fourth of six children, began writing poetry at the age of six. He won second place at the school oratorical contest at the age of ten. At that point, he decided that writing poetry was his ticket.

He was discouraged from writing at the age of eighteen when he was told his first book would never get published. Years later, he picked up his pen when his son asked why he had stopped writing and said he wanted to be able to write like his father. Now, at the age of forty-two, with seven children of his own, he is a happy father to have his children following in his footsteps as a writer and a poet.

Anthony hasn't put his pen down since.